D1008495

If the presence of God doesn't reach us in the dead of night,
rubbing our skin, like Jacob's, with sand
in a desert far from civilization,
then religion is simply a bunch of words. . . .

—Leslie Williams
NIGHT WRESTLING

NIGHT WRESTLING

NIGHT WRESTLING

~

*Struggling
for Answers and
Finding God*

by

Leslie Williams

WORD PUBLISHING
Dallas•London•Vancouver•Melbourne

PUBLISHED BY WORD PUBLISHING
Dallas, Texas

Night Wrestling: Struggling for Answers and Finding God. Copyright ©
1997 by Leslie Williams. All rights reserved. No portion of this book
may be reproduced, stored in a retrieval system, or transmitted in any
form or by any means—electronic, mechanical, photocopy, recording, or
any other—except for brief quotations in printed reviews, without the
prior permission of the publisher.

Library of Congress Cataloging-in-Publication Data
Williams, Leslie.
    Night wrestling : struggling for answers and finding God / by
Leslie Williams.
        p.   cm.
    Includes bibliographical references.
    ISBN 0-8499-1327-6
    1. Christian life—Episcopal authors.   2. Spiritual life—
Christianity.   3. Williams, Leslie.   I. Title.
BV4501.2.W5423   1997
248.4—dc21

96-48118
CIP

Printed in the United States of America
7 8 0 1 2 3 4 9 BVG 9 8 7 6 5 4 3 2 1

For my mother,
Mary-Allen Meriwether

Contents

Acknowledgments
XI

CHAPTER ONE
A Song for the Night Season
I

CHAPTER TWO
"The Lord Shall Be My God"
9

CHAPTER THREE
About Love
27

CHAPTER FOUR
Looking Back
51

CHAPTER FIVE
What Will Be . . .
79

CHAPTER SIX
Dust and Wind:
Spiritual Beings in Physical Bodies
103

CHAPTER SEVEN
Between Busyness and Loneliness:
Finding a Garden of Solitude
129

CHAPTER EIGHT
Death and Forgiveness
151

CHAPTER NINE
The Peace that Passes Understanding
175

Works Cited
193

Acknowledgments

First, I'd like to thank my husband, Stockton, for his support and encouragement, and my children, Jase and Caroline, for their patience and joy.

I'd also like to thank Floyd Thatcher for his wisdom and encouragement over the years; Bill Gohring for finding a home for this manuscript and for his wonderful sense of humor; Lucy Taft for her inspiration; Mary-Allen Meriwether, Sherry Hewett, Jim May, Jan Johnson, and Alyse Lounsberry for their editorial skill; Jane, Margie, Vickie, Jenness, Alison, Mary, and Pamela for encouraging my writing; Khris Ford for her spiritual direction at a crucial time in my life; and Kathy Parkis for her help during a computer crisis.

A big thank you goes to the first-rate staff at Word, especially Nelson Keener, whose insights have greatly improved this book.

Finally, I'd like to thank my family and my in-laws for their love and support over the years.

1

A Song for the Night Season

The Lord grants his loving kindness in the daytime; in the night
season his song is with me, a prayer to the God of my life.
—PSALM 42:10

When I picture Jacob wrestling all night with God, I see the two
of them nearly naked, thrashing around alone in the middle of
the desert, kicking up tufts of sand underneath a black, star-
speckled sky. Jacob's sweaty body glistens, muscles taut with
determination. He breathes heavily and seems exhausted. In spite
of his thigh wound, he refuses to let go of his opponent until he
receives a blessing. In the morning, as a majestic sunrise flares
across the desert sands, Jacob is rewarded: He has seen God face
to face. Though he limps, the glimpse of the Almighty has
changed his identity forever.

Jacob's story of the long night in the desert has often touched
me deeply. I have identified with Jacob's struggles in the dark, trying to recognize God, fighting against Him without knowing the
holiness of my opponent. In my spiritual journey, I have felt

attacked by things I don't understand and need to work through at the deepest level. For the last several years, my personal night-wrestling has taken place on a brown, faded couch in my living room. This old couch with the sunken center is where I have struggled with God, angels, demons, and other things that go bump in the night.

Several years ago, my husband, an Episcopal priest, answered a call to the soggy swamplands near Houston, Texas, where I spent five years and two months in a spiritual desert. Now that we have moved to Midland, an actual desert in West Texas, paradoxically I have emerged spiritually from that barren spot into a lush place where flowers are beginning to blossom again.

When we moved to Midland, I had the couch recovered. It was a fitting symbol of the passage from one spiritual stage into another. Recently, though, I found myself sleepless again, needing my old place to talk with God about a difficult problem. I stumbled into the den, dragging an afghan; then scrunching my pillow into shape, I was relieved to find that nothing about the couch had changed except the fabric. Instead of lying on a brown sofa with holes, I now stretched out on blue and gray stripes, but God was still there, waiting in the darkness, turning an ordinary couch into a giant-sized outstretched hand, big enough for me to curl up in.

As I think back about those many, many nights I spent in Houston whispering into what felt like empty darkness at the time, I now can thank God for those five years. During that time, God wrestled me to the ground, forcing me to die to the many destructive attitudes, painful memories, and selfish desires keeping me from Him.

Night after night I wrestled with questions that seemed to have no answers. My questions over the years have included the following: Why do so many of my relatives have to die in painful ways? Why, after seven years and three surgeries, can I bear no children? Why did my husband leave a comfortable profession in a town surrounded by family for a job that can't support us, in a place I can't get used to? What in God's name does He want with me anyway?

When I have spoken about these things to friends and to church groups, inevitably other questions arise, whispered privately by people with tears in their eyes. Why is my child gay? Why did my baby have to die? Why can I (or my spouse) not keep a job? Why does my husband abuse me? Why can I not find a husband (or a wife)?

I am writing to other night-wrestlers, people not content with pat answers, people combing the Bible and plunging deep into their faith to see the face of God and to find peace. A few of my personal questions now have answers; many still do not. But this book is not about answers. It is about the process of searching, and the glimmerings of hope found on the darkest of nights. It's about the gifts and blessings found in wrestling the death questions to the ground, and what God teaches us in spite of (or maybe *because* of) our pain. It's about the greatest blessing of all—intimacy with God.

Hope

In her poem "254," Emily Dickinson describes hope as a little feathery bird that chirps unceasingly in the soul. My image of hope is not nearly so profound or poetic as a soul-bird that refuses to quit singing. I visualize hope the way the movie producers created Tinkerbell in the Mary Martin version of *Peter Pan*. On the screen, she is an irregular speck of light, darting, flitting throughout the room, tinkling quietly instead of speaking directly, and coming from an unseen source. Hope is like that—inarticulate, emanating from God, and elusive.

Many times hope is confused with desire. For years I made this mistake in hoping for a child. Month by month, when my prayer was not realized, I felt that hope was a hoax, to be dashed against the wall of what was obviously "God's will." Gareth Jones, a Welsh priest and scholar, spoke on hope several years ago in Austin, Texas, calling it an "anchor of the Soul." Often considered the Cinderella of Christian virtues because she is ignored in favor of her sisters Faith and Love, Hope involves trust, endurance, and expectation. Gareth Jones used the example of Herman Lange, a German Christian executed under Hitler:

> When this letter comes to your hands, I shall no longer be among the living. The thing that has occupied our thoughts constantly for many months, never leaving them free, is now about to happen. If you ask me what state I am in, I can only answer, I am first in a joyous mood, and second, filled with great anticipation. As regards the first feeling, today means the end of all suffering and all earthly sorrow for me. As to the second feeling, this day brings the greatest hour of my life. . . . For me, believing will become seeing, hope will become possession. (93)

Hope will become possession. Fortunately, we don't have to be in prison awaiting execution to claim hope—although many times we build inner prisons from our own needs, demands, and expectations. Like love and faith, hope is a gift of the Spirit, sprinkled, or poured, or lavished on us even as we languish on an old brown couch in the middle of the night. It twinkles brightly, unexplainedly on the dark walls of our souls. It anchors us deep in Christ. The question is how to claim it.

Jacob's Story

> And Jacob was left alone; and a man wrestled with him until
> the breaking of the day. When the man saw that he did not
> prevail against Jacob, he touched the hollow of his thigh;
> and Jacob's thigh was put out of joint as he wrestled with
> him. Then he said, "Let me go, for the day is breaking." But
> Jacob said, "I will not let you go, unless you bless me." And
> he said to him, "What is your name?" And he said, "Jacob."
> Then he said, "Your name shall no more be called Jacob, but
> Israel, for you have striven with God and with men, and
> have prevailed." (Genesis 32:24–28)

Jacob's life was changed and he learned many things from his
night of wrestling. Along with the blessing from God, Jacob
received a new name. Jacob's new name was not a superficial
change in nomenclature; it also signified a new identity. Many of
us struggle in the middle of the night, wrestling with angels, trying to bring the events of our lives to the feet of God, trying to
wrest the blessing from the thing that seems about to destroy us.
When dawn breaks, when God's love and hope finally wash over
our exhausted spirits, then we, too, can claim a new identity.

Jacob didn't get away unscathed. The thigh wound inflicted by
God caused him to limp the rest of his life. We, too, are not the
same as we were before—we are wounded, scarred, marked,
changed, and we may walk forever with a limp. But we, too,
inherit the name "Israel." In addition, as Christians, we have a
gift that even Jacob as an Old Testament hero did not have. We
have the gift of the Holy Spirit to ease our pain, to empower us
to claim God's promises.

Gerard Manley Hopkins wrote a poem that asks some of the
same questions I have asked in the night. In "Carrion Comfort,"

Jacob feels his very bones are bruised and wonders why God has selected him. It feels as though he's being attacked by a lion. He just wants to get out of there and avoid the wrestling match altogether. At the end, both for Jacob in Hopkins' poem, and for us when the light finally dawns, the surprise is sprung: Though one night has felt like a year, it's God Himself who's been our opponent.

We might ask the same questions as Jacob: *Why me?* Our first reaction to suffering is often self-pity: We feel as though God has allowed life, like an arbitrary, uncaring shepherd, to grab us by the neck with a shepherd's crook, singling us out from the crowd for a particular lesson or for no particular reason at all. Like Jacob, we are frantic to avoid grappling, either with pain or with God. We don't understand why we have to suffer, why we have been served misery as our portion. Most of us would much rather move through life effortlessly, with answers to our deepest questions handed to us instead of wrung from God in what seems to be a fight to the death. However, with the dawn comes the realization that wrestling with God is a privilege, an opportunity to know Him in all His glory.

What Night-Wrestling Is About

In some ways, this book is a bridge between the inner spiritual journey (the private footpath through the landscape of the soul) and the external highway of life, where we are likely to have wrecks, or be stalled in traffic jams, or get lost. If we live in the real world, we cannot avoid the highway; but as Christians on a different kind of journey, we also need to exit, park, and meander the quieter pathways of the soul. I am continually searching for ways to integrate the experience of the highway into the experience of the soul. Besides including my own stories, this book compiles the signposts and tracks of fellow Christians throughout the centuries, as they have attempted to walk the solitary inner path with Jesus, integrating the outer journey into the soul's territory.

God comes to us wherever we are: in our toothaches, in the bittersweet pain of separation, in our kitchens filled with dirty dishes, in the howling, bleeding births of infants, in the still-births of dreams lost. God touches us, moves us, changes us in our nitty-gritty lives experienced by bodies capable of ripped flesh and souls that yearn for transcendence. If the presence of God doesn't reach us in the dead of night, rubbing our skin, like Jacob's, with sand in a desert far from civilization, then religion is simply a bunch of words.

This book is the story of struggle, and how hope and redemption fight off the disease of depression and despair that some people, in spite of firm belief, fall victim to during times of crisis. We are in good company. Most of the biblical heroes—Job, Jacob, Abraham, Jeremiah, to name a few—struggled with the meaning of faith and suffering. God reached deep into the well, literally at times, to rescue His loved ones, and He reaches deep into our souls to rescue us as well.

Getting through the night is sometimes rough, for Christians and non-believers alike. Jake Barnes, the macho hero of Hemingway's *The Sun Also Rises,* comments that it is easy to be hard-boiled in the daytime, but quite another thing at night. Our culture lures us with false promises of hope in dark times—drinking, sex, drugs, and other, more subtle but titillating death-toys dangled temptingly before us on billboards, TV ads, media presentations, and in our cultural undercurrent.

Surviving the night, getting through the tough times, requires a different approach from anything the culture provides. William Law, speaking to us across several centuries, offers an alternative discipline for the night.

Represent to your imagination that your bed is your grave; that all things are ready for your interment; that you are to have no more to do with this world; and that it will be owing to God's great mercy if you ever see the light of the sun again or have another day to add to your works of piety. Then commit yourself to sleep as one that is to have no more opportunities of doing good, but is to awake among spirits that are separate from the body and waiting for the judgment of the last great day.

Such a solemn resignation of yourself into the hands of God every evening, and parting with all the world as if you were never to see it any more—and all this in the silence and darkness of the night—is a practice that will soon have excellent effects upon your spirit. For this time of the night is exceeding proper for such prayers and meditations. (151)

Night *Wrestling* explores the spiritual implications of giving God control of our lives, dealing with issues such as our past, our future, materialism, death, forgiveness, and peace.

Having spent so many nights awake and struggling on the old brown couch, my hope is that this book will be a song for the night season for other fellow night-wrestlers.

Keep watch, dear Lord, with those who work, or watch, or weep this night, and give your angels charge over those who sleep. Tend the sick, Lord Christ; give rest to the weary, bless the dying, soothe the suffering, pity the afflicted, shield the joyous; and all for your love's sake. Amen.

(THE BOOK OF COMMON PRAYER, *page 134*)

2

"The Lord
Shall Be My God"

Were the whole realm of nature mine,
that were an offering far too small;
love so amazing, so divine,
demands my soul, my life, my all.
—Isaac Watts (1674–1748)

In Robert Browning's poem, "Pippa Passes," young Pippa has one day off a year from a cruel, slave-like job at the Asolo woolen mills. One year on her holiday, she skips merrily through the town, singing the famous line, "God's in his heaven—All's right with the world!" What most people don't realize is the irony in Browning's line. In the poem, Pippa passes four groups of people involved in murder, adultery, lies, and betrayal. Though her innocence influences their evil for good, we cannot take her saying at face value. By the end of the poem, Browning's message emerges: Just because God's in His heaven doesn't mean everything is all right with the world.

In fact, there are times when it seems that God's not even in His heaven, that nobody is in control. With murder, adultery, lies, and betrayal on the loose in the world, who is watching out for us? In what seems to be a void, we often try to take control, playing God in our lives and the lives of others.

Many people find the issue of control difficult, especially when it comes to a God who works in mysterious, not obvious, ways. Because when we are children we can control so little growing up, as adults we believe at our deepest level that determining our lives—from the big things like deciding where we live and what we do, to the small things like the arrangement of figurines on the mantle—will bring happiness and peace. If the chaos of a difficult childhood didn't bring us happiness and peace, then the manipulation, regulation, and command of our own lives must be the answer.

Wrong. But by the time we reach adulthood, the desire for most of us to order our own existence has been set in concrete foundations. We may give lip-service to "giving our lives to the Lord," but at a deeper level, we are wrestling for power, just like Jacob.

Rayford High, an Episcopal priest at St. Paul's Church in Waco, preached a thought-provoking sermon once on what it takes to give your life to Christ. Jesus said, "Take up your cross and follow me." Rayford interpreted the passage something like this: Taking up your cross doesn't mean that you'd be willing to shoulder inconveniences in order to follow Christ. Taking up your cross means heaving an enormous, heavy instrument of death onto your back and hauling it up a hill. That alone takes all your strength. The next step is to stick the cross in a hole in the ground, climb up on it, and die.

As I know from my own experience, we don't like to think too hard about this saying of Jesus. Where is all the feel-good stuff about becoming a Christian? Where is the joy? Where are all the benefits? The quip, "No cross, no crown," suddenly takes on a new, potent meaning. Most of us are not fully prepared to die to self on the cross before we taste the benefits of Christianity.

So what did Rayford mean? I don't think he meant we have to be crucified literally in order to follow Christ. I think he meant we have to die to ourselves and our plans and our desires in order to be true disciples. If we do, then the reward is Easter and a sumptuous banquet, and joy and love radiating at a higher wattage than we can imagine. Yet, I think Rayford—and Jesus—were both deadly serious about dying to our old ways.

This means that when we give our lives to Jesus, we give Him the control. To me, this feels like dying. And I die hard, fighting clear through the night, like Jacob. As each new control issue comes up, I still wrestle, even though I know better.

After all, isn't it my life?

In his book, *The God Who Comes*, Carlo Carretto describes why faith is so difficult and how we struggle against belief:

> Only very late do we learn the price of the risk of believing, because only very late do we face up to the idea of death.
>
> This is what is difficult: Believing truly means dying. Dying to everything: to our reasoning, to our plans, to our past, to our childhood dreams, to our attachment to earth, and sometimes even to the sunlight, as at the moment of our physical death. (21)

Because we give up everything to Jesus, even our lives, faith is the ultimate relinquishment of control.

Greek literature, especially the drama, is filled with the tension between destiny (fate) and choice. Just how much control do we have over our lives? Even those with the greatest amount of earthly power, heroes such as King Oedipus, still fall prey to the will of the gods. One of the great questions in the play *Oedipus Rex* is this: What role did Oedipus, with his tragic flaws of pride and anger, play in his own downfall? In other words, to what extent was his tragedy unavoidable?

We might ask the same questions of our own lives. How often do our stubbornness, our pride, and our anger bring about a personal debacle—and how often does God have to redeem a mess we've gotten ourselves into? Who is in control anyway? And to what degree can we choose to shape our destiny? The difference between Oedipus' dilemma and ours is that the Greeks believed in arbitrary and petty gods, while the Christian God who shapes our lives does so for our ultimate benefit.

My Struggle with Control

The first time I thought about control as a personal, spiritual issue was when I suddenly didn't have any, after I'd set up my adult life, thinking everything was going my way. As a child, I lived in nineteen houses by the time I was twenty-one. Some of them felt like home, but some of them belonged to other people and were furnished with their special things, not ours. As an adult, the idea of home has been an obsession. When I was twenty-five, I moved back to the town where I graduated from high school and married one of my old buddies from World Geography class, an attorney with roots in the community three generations deep. I was safe at last, controlling my own destiny.

But no. God called my husband away from lawyering into the ordained ministry. I dropped my own course of study at the seminary in Austin, and we spent three years in Alexandria, Virginia. I worked on Capitol Hill in the State of Texas office. Then we moved to St. Paul's in Waco, where we adopted our long-awaited son, and where at long last (age thirty-eight) I picked up my studies in Baylor's Ph.D. program, combining religion and literature.

A week into my second semester there, I burst into our kitchen. "Oh, Stockton!" I bubbled like a kid. "This class is sent by God! It's bringing together the last eighteen years of all my studies!"

My husband responded, "That's great." Pause. "The bishop called."

Within a month, we moved from Waco to Houston, a city I had always avoided. I'd even joked, "Stockton, I'll follow you anywhere except Alaska or Houston." In spite of my gut-level despair and resistance, we headed straight for the jaws of a steel-and-glass monster-city with skyscrapers my two-year-old called "dinosaurs," and freeway traffic that would kill you if you sneezed at the wheel.

We moved during Lent. A good friend asked what I had given up for my Lenten discipline. I replied in a feeble attempt to make light of the situation, "Well, I decided to give up my friends, my church, my degree program, my house, my town, my security. I guess I could add chocolate to the list, but I think that's enough for one season."

Every Wednesday afternoon I cried, picturing my fellow students seated around the conference table at Baylor engaged in lively and meaningful discussion, while I sewed curtains. (I hate sewing. I hate curtains. But we couldn't afford to buy them, so there I was.) Pushing the iron over blue tropical birds and green swirls for the guest room, I thought, *Boy, if this were my life, I'd sure be living it differently.*

The iron stopped, steam hissing from the little holes in the hot bottom.

This is your life.

If this realization weren't bad enough, the second one made me unplug the iron. *No, it's not. You gave your life to Jesus, remember? He must have thought you were serious.*

Thus began my great struggle over whose life it was, anyway, and what I wanted out of it, versus what Christ wanted—which were clearly two different things.

Who Gets to Be the Boss?

When Jacob dedicated his life to God, here were his terms: "If God will be with me, and will keep me in this way that I go, and will give me bread to eat and clothing to wear, so that I come again to my father's house in peace, then the Lord shall be my God" (Genesis 28:20–21). I find the word *if* very interesting. Like the rest of us, Jacob had a lot to learn about a covenant with God— that we cannot control the terms of the contract or the circumstances of our lives, and that once we claim the Lord as our God, we belong to Him and not vice-versa.

The idea of control carries with it several aspects, all extremely attractive and tempting. No wonder Jacob refused to let go. Even Jesus was tempted with this one. In the wilderness, the devil offered not just power, but control—the determination of His life and others'. Also, on the cross, the crowd taunted Him. Even at that point, He could have taken His life in His own hands and decided not to go through with God's plan. This very issue is what Gethsemane was all about. Jesus could easily have controlled His own destiny. He could have opted for ten more years of ministry, with every reason to believe the extra time would increase His effectiveness. Instead, He said, "Your will, not mine," and died.

Who calls the shots? Who makes the plans? Who decides on the timing? Who gets to be the boss? I have always rejoiced in God's will when it coincides with what I want; but alone in that house in Houston, I grieved. Deep in my heart, I wanted to be the boss. I wanted to make my own plans for my life. I wanted to snatch my life back from the gentle hands of God and hold it to my chest, growling, "I've changed my mind. I don't really like what You've planned for me."

The problem is, when you give your life to Christ, He takes it. You can't just loan it to Him, and you can't play catch with Him: Now it's His, now it's mine. The questions become, *How serious am I? Am I willing to make a contract, like a marriage, or do I prefer a breezier arrangement, to come and go in the relationship like a live-in with no strings? To give Jesus control means that I trust Him.*

And look where that's gotten me, the grump inside me replies.

After we moved to Houston, our lives avalanched straight downhill with the force of snow barreling down a mountainside. My brother-in-law, Tom, lived with us off and on for a year because he was fighting cancer and being treated at M. D. Anderson. We lost every cent we had because our house in Waco didn't sell. Our adoption agency was running behind, month after anxious month. I developed acute asthma. As the situation deteriorated, I kept thinking, *Trust. God's plan. Hmmmm.*

During those early months, I would lie on the brown couch in the dark, listening to Tom cough, praying that he would wake up in the morning, that my son wouldn't toddle in to play with "Uncle Tong" and find him lifeless. Tom struggled with the same issues I did—trust and control. Only he faced real death and excruciating pain instead of mere disappointment. I felt guilty because my problems were minor in comparison to his. Yet my guilt and my focus on Tom ultimately didn't stop the necessity of coming to terms with the issue of God's control. In fact, watching Tom struggle brought the issue of control to an almost unbearably poignant head.

Our living room faced the street, and at two in the morning the streetlamp's light trickled in, creating shadows that skittered when the occasional car drove by. "Lord," I said to the bookcases and the coffee table, "if You'll just tell me why we're here, why Tom has to suffer like this, why I had to leave Baylor and what I thought was Your plan for me, why our house won't sell, why the baby isn't coming, why I can't breathe, I could be satisfied. Maybe I could get some sleep."

The Silence of God

One of the most terrifying sounds of the twentieth century has been the noise of an atomic explosion. A sound just as terrifying, though, has ricocheted off the earth for centuries at one time or another in the lives of Christians: the silence of God. The last question I whispered into the shadows of our Houston living room was, "Why are You silent? I can bear even the other things, except Your silence." Gradually, I'd fall asleep in the stillness, deep as a tomb.

During the day, I tried to support my husband, who'd been sent to this church to rescue it. Barely four years old, the mission had been founded on cracked bedrock, and two divergent and determined groups had a death-grip on the controls. This was my husband's first assignment on his own, and neither of us had ever seen the nastiness of a church fight. I refused to get in the middle, having deep affection for people on both sides. Desperate for a place to worship without turmoil, I used to sneak off to the Roman Catholic church a mile away. *Lord,* I prayed, *I have followed my husband like a good wife. I have given up what I thought You wanted me to do. But I can't survive without Your church. You can't take away my church too.*

Silence.

Then Tom died. Then other family members started dying. "Be Thou My Vision" became the theme song for many funerals during the next four-and-a-half years. I prayed, *Lord, how many loved ones are You going to take?*

Silence.

I prayed, *Lord, I don't mind giving my plans to You, but I need to feel that You are in control, that I'm not just a speck of dust in a whirlwind of fate.*

Silence.

God must have known I was fibbing. I *did* mind giving up *my* plans to Him. I was still trying to be the boss. I had tried with all *my* strength to save Tom. I prayed with all *my* heart to save the others. I still wanted to control *my* destiny, to fulfill *my* vocation for Christ.

Original Sin

Several years passed. Our house finally sold. Our baby girl arrived, a dimpled beauty well worth waiting for. I entered another Ph.D. program, this time at the University of Houston. By the time we moved to Midland, the church was a thriving parish, seven hundred strong. My two children were healthy and happy. I had also managed to give warily to the Lord what was His in the first place—control of my life.

God, in all His wisdom, kept quiet until I finally heard the high-pitched "me, me, me, me" in all my prayers. He sent me to a sensitive spiritual adviser, who helped me see that silence is a great purifier, not a denial of love and concern. The self, with its stranglehold on life, is what must die before we can be free. God really *does* have plans better than ours, but we can't live them out until we get rid of the self.

The whole idea that our lives belong to us is a myth, and an arrogant assumption when it comes right down to it. I did not conceive myself; I wasn't my own idea. I cannot will myself to wake up in the mornings—it is by God's grace alone that I am given even one more day to live.

Giving God control of my life became much easier once I realized He already had it.

One night I dreamed there was a woman who lived in my basement, a wart-covered, slobbering hag with witch-like grasping fingers and greasy hair. She was the one screaming, "Me, me, me, me." She was unattractive, untouchable. Hideous. When I woke up, I realized she was the one who lusted after control, howling and throwing things when she didn't get her way.

She is the one beneath the pious front, the self I hide from myself, the cellar-creature Christ died for. Once I realized how base I really am, then the miracle became not that I was able to give my life to Christ, *but that He was willing to take it.*

That sort of puts a different spin on giving up control of our lives. What would we do if God didn't want us? What would we become if He had refused to redeem our basement selves?

Early during the same night that Jacob wrestled with the angel, he reached a point of deep humility, recognizing that he was not worthy of the steadfast love and all the faithfulness God had shown him: "I am not worthy" (Genesis 32:10). Yet his humility did not stop him from taking on the man who wrestled with him. Even as we realize how lost we'd be without God, we still seem to have the need to fight for our rights.

In developing the idea of original sin, St. Augustine in *Confessions* gives the image of himself as a squalling baby, enraged when he did not get his needs met immediately. "And if my wishes were not carried out . . . I would take my revenge by bursting into tears" (25, 26). At the very center of original sin is the desire to get our way, to have life on our own terms. As we go through life, this impulse remains intact; we simply become more sophisticated than a screaming infant with flailing arms.

God's Larger Plan

Hindsight is a mixed blessing, of course, a double-edged gift: Just when you finally understand what all that was about, it's too late to use the knowledge—at least for that go-around. Out of the last five years, I learned a few things I wished I'd known before; but if I'm honest, I probably wouldn't have paid attention at the time. Like Dorothy in *The Wizard of Oz,* who asked Glenda, "Why didn't you tell me this before?"—I had to learn it for myself.

The first thing I had to recognize about God's control versus my control is that He is working from a larger plan. Whereas I am limited by my selfish perspective (tunnel vision), and a straight-jacket of security needs, God sees the whole plan. He sees how our lives cross paths with others', both now and also around the bend, where we can't see. He places us in situations, not for our own benefit, but for the benefit of others. While we're stumbling around in the desert getting sand between our toes and whining like the Israelites, sometimes it helps to realize we have been placed where we are as the answer to someone else's prayers. As my sister said, "I know why you were sent to Houston. So Tom would have a place to stay." Who knows? Sometimes we are seemingly destroyed in order for God to build something more wonderful within. We're just too busy sulking to see it.

Beauty from Brokenness

My husband gave a sermon illustration once, a story he heard from a source he can't remember. A famous potter created unique kinds of pots, each one different, with irregular map-like shapes outlined with gold rivulets. These pots began to sell for a high price, and someone asked the potter one day what his secret was. "Well," he answered, "first I make an ordinary pot, glaze it, and fire it. Then I take a hammer and smash it into many pieces."

"You smash your creation?" asked the visitor, incredulous.

"Yes." The potter smiled. "Then I solder the pieces together with liquid gold, and the new creation is stronger and more beautiful than the original."

When God smashes our plans, what we see are the pieces of our lives and our selves lying about on the floor. We grieve for the old pot. What we often don't see is how He is also busy soldering us back together into a beautiful new creation.

God as a Kind but Firm Parent

The second thing I learned about God's control and the necessity of trusting Him is obvious, but bears repeating. Like a parent who knows that too much candy makes you throw up, God hides the chocolate drops just when we think we will die if we don't get some. Any parent knows the frustrating feeling of trying to explain to a screaming child, "I'm doing this for your own good." Most parents know more than most four-year-olds (although some days, when I've been outwitted, I wonder); and we must assume that God knows more than we do.

In Houston, even though I knew better, I was the screaming child. I simply could not believe that God had my best interests in mind. Like a good parent-child relationship, trust has to be developed so that even though we are disappointed about the chocolate, we understand (as we mature in the faith) that it is for our sake it is denied. Every time I have pushed for my own will over what I suspected God wanted me to do (in matters where I really did have some control), I have gotten sick one way or another. For instance, although I'm getting better about not taking on too many commitments, I still take on more than I know I should because I want to, rather than asking prayerfully whether the Lord wants me to or not.

God's in Control, Even When It Doesn't Feel Like It

The third thing I noticed about God's control is that sometimes it doesn't feel as though He's in control. It doesn't feel as though He's home. It doesn't feel as though He's anywhere in the universe. Instead of the warm, cozy feeling of being sent an up-to-date map by a friendly AAA agent, God's *modus operandi* sometimes feels like being kicked out on your behind in a sandstorm with a broken compass. For those of us stuck in the control mode, it's important to feel that somebody has the power to do something, *anything*. A wrong direction feels better than no direction. If the leader isn't doing a good job, then the temptation to take over is too great, even if it leads to destruction.

Coupled with this desperation to *do* something, the great American myth of independence controls our attitudes subliminally. In this country, we pull ourselves up by our own bootstraps; we are self-made people; we will not tolerate the frightened passivity necessary to wait out a storm of confusion. Action. Control. Take your life in your own hands. Giving over the important decisions to a higher power is anathema, especially when it feels as though the higher power is on an extended lunch break.

If someone had come to me for spiritual advice ten years ago, I could have said what I have just written. These insights are not original, not complicated. However, the difference is that before, I would have been reciting an abstract script learned from Bible study and seminary.

Now, like the male character in Flannery O'Connor's short

story "Parker's Back," who had religious images and words tattooed all over his body, these truths are no longer external; this knowledge has been etched into my body, painted permanently. It has become a part of me.

One of the central reasons I feel that God sometimes plays havoc with our plans is so that we will take the theology we know with only our minds, and make this theology a part of our experience. We move from saying glibly, "I gave my life to Jesus," to lying on the table allowing God to inscribe His words on us. The process of claiming our faith is painful. It takes a long time. Often, we wish we were somewhere different, doing anything else. In this process, though, God moves from being the Other, the Holy distant One, to becoming a part of us. We are marked, like Jacob, by wrestling. And we are rewarded beyond our wildest dreams.

Trust

How do we get there? The common thread between these three insights is trust. Control issues are really trust issues. I remember sitting on my bed in May of seventh grade. I had survived the jungle of a new junior high school, and finally gotten an invitation to a party. Unfortunately, we were moving a few days before the party, so I wouldn't be able to go. Mother came into my room to comfort me. "There will be other parties at Leakey. You already know Linda, and you know how she loves to dance."

The argument did not take away the tight constriction around my chest, the feeling of anger, of helplessness, of desperation to go to the party. All right. There might be parties at Leakey. But would I be invited to them? For a year, I had battled an army of adolescent girls with cute clothes, make-up, and insider snickering, who deliberately ostracized me from the lunch table. There had been many parties I had not been invited to. Now I would have to repeat the battle again. And again. And again.

Like many men in the fifties and sixties—before parenting roles began to be shared—my father based his decisions to move on his own vocational interests, without understanding the effects that repeated mobility had on children. Though I understand him better now, as a teen, I felt I couldn't trust him to keep my best interests in mind. As an adult, the lack of trust has been difficult to shake: How could I trust God either, when the helplessness of being moved against my will as an adult felt identical to this helplessness of my teen years?

At some point on my couch in Houston, I accepted the fact that God was trustworthy. True, the only father-pattern I had was not ideal, but I finally bought the idea that God isn't like that. At first, this insight was an idea. It wasn't a feeling. Then, as I asked repeatedly for God to chisel a path from my brain to my heart, gradually, gradually, I allowed myself to relax the white-knuckled grip I had on my desire to control my life.

Building trust at this level was like building a stalagmite in a cave of fear. God slowly, slowly dripped reassurances on the rocky floor until a tiny bud of a formation began to show. I have known people for whom trust in God has grown into a solid rock column: Drop by drop, God's love has built up the trust so that the stalagmite reaches the source of water and connects directly.

During this trust-building process, several things helped. First, I asked directly for the *feeling* of trust. There was no problem with the faith in my head. There was a big problem with faith in my stomach. I asked God for relief in the stomach—gut-faith, heart-faith, faith I could feel in my body at the cellular level. Head-faith wasn't enough.

Second, I took heart from the Israelites. Although I would like to see myself as the apostle John in his constancy and his love for the Lord, I know myself to be closer to the psalmist who laments, "How long, O Lord?" (Psalm 13). As a result, I scoured the psalms for inspiration, and discovered how the Israelites, when they were in exile, or discouraged, repeated the stories of when the Lord had been faithful to them, when He had delivered them from their distress. Over and over the psalms tell the story of deliverance from Egypt. Over and over they tell of the Lord's goodness. The litany of past glories was a great help in the dark times.

In response, I formed my own litany of times the Lord has pulled through in my life, even when I thought He wouldn't. The story of how I met and fell in love with Stockton; the story of when we picked up our radiant children from the Gladney Center in Fort Worth; the stories of how I had found various jobs at just the right time; the story of how one family member "saved" us all by going into treatment for substance abuse. By repeating over and over the personal redemption stories from my own life, trust and love began to grow.

It is often tempting to water the old plants of fear and untrust. To choose deliberately to water new plants of faith, to forge new pathways in the brain and in the soul, takes monumental effort— and a power greater than my own will. No way could I simply have decided to trust. Not with my background. Not with my personality. The weeds from my past took over every time.

"When I grow up, I'm going to run my life MY way." This statement of survival from my childhood had become a soul-strangling guideline. As long as I lived by that creed, I crippled my life in God—and probably crippled my potential as a person along the way. Only the conscious repetition of God's redeeming acts in my life, combined with instant and constant prayer from the moment those fearful thoughts weasel in—only then can the Holy Spirit continue to build the trust necessary to allow God to control my life as *He* sees fit.

Accepting Death of Ourselves

Finally, Tom gave us all a parting gift. We can live only when we accept death, either death to the body in his case, or death to our plans or to our inner selves. This is, of course, deeply biblical, and we all recognize this abstract truth. However, to witness first-hand the drama of death played out, to watch a healthy man shrink to a cadaverous weight, to watch a person with a genius IQ being reduced to a blithering human being, broke my heart. By loving Tom, when he died, we were all partially smashed, like the potter's pot, but he was blasted apart into a million pieces. Yet, right before he died, Tom accepted his death, and it was as though the Holy Spirit swooped down with a crowd of angels and lifted him from the bed. Though we cannot see it, there is a pot in heaven wrought with pure gold.

In his death, Tom glorified God. Tom taught me that whatever God's plan is for us, even if it involves allowing the world's natural forces to overtake the physical body, even then can we glorify God. Tom is out of pain. He has gone home. He understands the "why's" that still torment us so. The line from Job comes to mind, ironically because Tom was working on a book about Job: "Though he slay me, yet will I trust in Him" (Job 13:15, KJV).

We cannot control our lives past a certain level even if we want to. Our lives are God's, to give or take as He sees fit. Tom's life and death, and my own experience, have taught me that I should wake up every morning and say, "Thank You for the ride. Thank You for one more day."

Of course, I still have times on the couch in the night. Now, though, instead of the cold, hard blackness of obsidian surrounding me, I see occasional flickerings of light on the wall. I know that God's silence does not mean His absence, and that if I'm patient and listen, soon I will hear what He's trying to teach me.

After the vision of the angels ascending into heaven on a ladder, Jacob gave his life to God when he was on a religious high, as so many of us do. Whether we express it or not, we expect blessings from God, and our own expectations and agendas undergird our commitment. Then God allows circumstances to test us, and He sends not an angel of comfort but an angel of power to wrestle with us until we are able to give Him our lives more completely, without the attached agendas. Only when we have done this work of wrestling in an ultimate power struggle can we be truly His.

Though we never walk the same again and some, like Tom, die, the blessings we receive are deeper than we know how to ask for. One of these blessings is the ability to love—ourselves and others.

I am the resurrection and the life, saith the Lord;
he that believeth in me, though he were dead, yet shall he live;
and whosoever liveth and believeth in me shall never die. . . .
For none of us liveth to himself,
and no man dieth to himself.
for if we live, we live unto the Lord;
and if we die, we die unto the Lord.
Whether we live, therefore, or die, we are the Lord's.

(THE BOOK OF COMMON PRAYER, *page 469*)

3

About Love

One who can love oneself loves all people.
—St. Anthony of Egypt

Eleven years ago during Lent, I found myself hurtling in a rented car through the Arizona desert at dawn, escaping after two days from Family Week at the Meadows Treatment Center. Because I was the dutiful and responsible child, I had gone to the treatment center to "help" a family member. I personally was fine, of course, because I'd learned the secret to life early on. I'd internalized the list of appropriate behaviors, and I planned to spend the rest of my life checking them off. With a few—but conspicuous—black marks, my chart already glowed in the dark with all the checks. I was therefore having a measurably successful life—and as I barreled out of Wickenburg, Arizona as fast as I could, I honestly thought the treatment center was trying to rip off me and my family with a bunch of hooey.

The drive from Wickenburg to the airport in Phoenix takes an hour, through a lonely landscape that looks like miles and miles of kitty litter with families of saguaro cactus hunkered down in it. That morning I traveled toward the dawn's deep rose, then coral, then lavender, and finally blue backdrop. About halfway to the Phoenix airport, I pulled over to the side of the road, weeping. Something was wrong. I knew God loved me, but *I'd never really felt His love.* Instead of the confident matron with the clipboard, I suddenly saw myself as a street urchin begging love like loose change tossed my way. I knew I needed inner healing, but felt I didn't deserve to be that happy.

Finally, the grace of God convinced me that I was worth the trouble. What actually clinched the argument was not the flutter of angel wings, but realizing that this week was already paid for, and I was neck-deep in a family system so sick it would cost more than my life savings to get me fixed if I didn't turn around right now. God knew me well enough to know what would finally make me wrench the steering wheel around and go back.

The recovery movement has helped many of us become aware of why God's love is so hard to accept and why we have difficulty loving ourselves. That family week at the Meadows was one long AHA! as I learned about my own disease in recovery terms. The shame core and low self-esteem I "inherited" distanced me from God's love, and forced me to try to earn my way instead of accepting God's grace offered freely.

Yet this spiritual problem of accepting God's love goes beyond recovery, deep into our natures, back to the Garden of Eden. It goes back to when Adam and Eve originally rebelled against God, making the intentional decision to do something they knew would cause death and alienate themselves from God. Tempted to be as smart as God, Adam and Eve *chose* to put the relationship with God at odds—we humans, not God, ruined things.

They then hid themselves because they were ashamed, feeling for the first time their unworthiness.

Centuries later, even after God paid the debt for our sinful mistakes by dying on the cross, we still struggle. We still hide in the bushes, naked. Because of our fallen natures, God's gift of unconditional love is sometimes like those prickly saguaro cacti in bloom: stunning to look at, but painful to pick up with bare hands, and far too prickly to transplant into our own backyards.

Accepting God's Love

Making the commitment to give our lives to Christ and struggling to give up the job of ringmaster is one thing. Allowing ourselves to experience—to celebrate, to rest in, to dance in, to luxuriate in—God's love is another. Here's the dilemma: On the one hand, nobody is worthy of Christ's love, nobody is esteemed enough in his or her own right to deserve His sacrifice on the cross. On the other hand, to wallow in our unworthiness is a slap in the face of God, a rejection of the greatest gift in the world. The trick is to accept the gift of worthiness, with humility, even when we know we don't deserve it.

Other questions arise as well. If I accept God's gift to become whole, why do I still feel insecure in my relationships? Why do I still sometimes get depressed? Why do I sometimes still feel like a failure as a person?

The problem is, we are mesmerized into believing that we, or something in the world, can make the difference in our happiness. We look to the material world to heal a spiritual problem.

Acceptance of Christ's love demands that we grow in love toward ourselves, toward others, toward God. We can't help it. On the other hand, old habits of non-love die hard. Our souls are grooved like recorded disks, forced to play the same sad music over and over and over unless a power greater than we are forces a dramatic change.

We need to remember that God thought we were worth saving when Christ died on the cross, and He still thinks we are worth saving. At one level, we accept this gift with joy, but at a deeper level perhaps, we shy away. Many of us have built spiritual lives in tent cities, scrounging cardboard and other scraps for shelter because we feel we are not worthy to live in the Beverly Hills of Christ's kingdom.

Jacob's Story

The Bible does not give us a reading on Jacob's feelings of worthiness the night he wrestled with God. Encouraged by his mother, he must have felt fairly self-confident of God's affirmation when he tricked his brother out of his inheritance. The night he wrestled, though, he might have been having second thoughts. He faced the same angry brother's army the next morning, and one wonders whether he was feeling insecure about his actions years before, or even wondering whether he deserved God's blessings or not.

I see two connections between Jacob's story and our difficulty in learning how to love God and accept God's love. First, on the eve of Jacob's encounter with his brother, his whole identity in God's eyes and in his own is called into question. Instead of being the blessed one, his existence is threatened with annihilation. Alone in the dark desert, God does not choose to give him an uplifting vision as He had before with the dream of the ladder ascending to heaven, or to tap him on the shoulder and whisper, "Don't worry. You're okay." Instead, He sends a powerful and tenacious antagonist, and Jacob is forced to wrestle for his life. This is not a "warm fuzzy" experience from God.

The feelings of unworthiness can be powerful and tenacious. Once we commit our lives to God, our childhood scars do not automatically heal, nor do we blossom into perfect Christians overnight. Instead, undoing psychological and emotional damage often takes longer than it took for the injuries to be inflicted in the first place. However, God is as tenacious in healing us as He was in dealing with Jacob. He will not let go of us until He has blessed us. Although it sometimes seems as if our sense of being unlovable is more persistent, more powerful than our ability to accept love, God will win in the long run, if we continue to wrestle and pray.

Second, Jacob knew he was fighting to the death with a strong adversary. At dawn, when he discovered the identity of his partner in battle, he must have been surprised. He'd been in the arms of God all night, and he—Jacob—was the adversary. In dealing with problems of worth, we need to realize that *we* are the problem, and God is wrestling *with us*, not against us. Our human sin and sickness instigate the conflict, and though it feels like a fight to the death, we never leave the arms of God.

Frankenstein

Mary Shelley's Frankenstein has captured our cultural imagination for almost two centuries—the terrible/pitiable square face of Boris Karloff's monster haunts our dreams. I find that this story helps explore the intricate interconnection of love. *Frankenstein* illuminates the paradox that we cannot love others until we love ourselves and that we cannot love ourselves until we have been loved by others or by God. The monster's heart-wrenching search for love from others and from his creator represents both the desperation we feel when the quest is foiled and the resulting destruction caused by a lack of love. Three different interpretations have helped me understand the process.

Our *"Dark" Side vs. Our "Rational" Side*

First, since 1816 when Mary Shelley first published her story, Dr. Frankenstein and his monster have been viewed as being two sides of the same person—one consciousness with both a "dark" side and a "rational" side. Psychologists have had a heyday with this idea, of course, promoting the notion that such a split ultimately leads to insanity (or death, in Dr. Frankenstein's case) if we cannot integrate the two parts of our personalities.

For Christians, acceptance of the monster part of ourselves is imperative. If we pretend the dark side doesn't exist, or if we try to push it away, the dark side comes out in another form. If we ignore this side of ourselves, then pride in our own goodness is what sustains us, and we think we do not need either forgiveness or grace. In addition, when we ignore the monster part of us, it makes us prone to point the finger at all those "Frankensteins" among us.

Dr. Frankenstein dies without acknowledging and accepting the monster he has created. The poor creature chases after him, begging for love, then, when he doesn't receive it, goes away raging and killing off Dr. Frankenstein's family and friends, one by one, in revenge. If Dr. Frankenstein had loved his monster instead of rejecting him, the violence may not have occurred. Dr. Frankenstein says, "[We] are enemies. Begone, or let us try our strength in a fight, in which one must fall." The monster replies, "How can I move thee? Will no entreaties cause thee to turn a favorable eye upon thy creature, who implores goodness and compassion?" (96)

Like Frankenstein's monster, an unaffirmed, unacknowledged dark side ultimately causes great damage. Like Frankenstein's monster, often the dark side gains strength over the rational side, and sooner or later causes the death of something precious.

Christ did not come to redeem us from our strengths, but from our dark sides.

The biblical parallel is in Matthew, Luke, and Mark: "Every kingdom divided against itself is laid waste, and no city or house divided against itself will stand" (Matthew 12:25). Jesus is talking to the scribes who accuse him of using Satan to cast out demons. Jesus' reply is, "Why should Satan work against himself? His house would surely fall." Commentators for centuries have known that unity is strength. *The Interpreter's Bible* says that the

> assertion of the necessity of unified personality, as making for stability, for mental and spiritual wholeness, was an insight which mental hygiene, after many centuries has strongly underlined and amplified. (692)

James called the divided will "war in your members" (James 4:1).

We cannot, by our own will, live only in the light or unify ourselves. Our natures are not pure. Because we are fallen beings, we create monsters out of bad motives, evil thoughts, envy, lust—you name it. The answer to a unified soul is not to ignore our sins, to rebuff our "monsters," but to accept them and ask God to forgive us for allowing them to rant and rave and wreak damage in our lives. Yes, the house will fall if we remain divided. The way to rid ourselves of the monsters is to acknowledge them and give them to God, who can then cleanse our natures.

Looking in the Mirror

An example from my own life occurred during the trial of one of two young men who murdered my aunt, uncle, and cousin. During Sunday supper, these two kids high on drugs had forced their way into my relatives' home and beaten them to death with a tire iron and a cedar post. Our family had spent over a year in grief and horror at the kind of sub-human person who could commit such a terrible act.

The trial of the second young man consisted of the defense attorney and a wealthy psychiatrist proving to the jury that the poor guy couldn't help his violent and premeditated actions because he was "depressed."

I became so angry that I wanted to take the murder weapon lying on the display table and beat the young man to death right there in the courtroom.

I meant it.

Of course, I didn't follow through. However, the night after the trial—spent again wrestling on the couch—I wept, as I had for a year for my relatives, but this night I also wept for something new: the lost image of myself as a kind, Christian woman. I did not turn the other cheek. I wanted to pulverize that smirking, greasy-haired kid, who turned around and stared down my mother in the courtroom.

That night, when I looked in the mirror, I saw the basement hag again, looking just like Frankenstein's monster. Instead of my own pious image, I saw the face of the murderer. God's grace, my family's love, the values in my upbringing, and the choices I had made were all that separated me from that murderer. Inside, I was potentially no better than he.

This recognition of my inner monster allowed me to ask for forgiveness for my own deadly thoughts and impulses. It also (eventually) allowed me to begin to pray for the tortured souls of those two boys.

In his book *Prayers for the Breaking of Bread: Meditations on the Collects of the Church Year,* Herbert O'Driscoll discusses the "mingling of light and darkness," and the necessity of allowing them to mix instead of being separated:

Mysteriously my light and my darkness is one. I am not two beings, one wonderfully full of light, the other a rather horrible pool of darkness! In fact my wholeness as a human being depends on my bringing my whole self before God and offering its light and darkness. . . . I begin to discover the glorious, liberating, and energizing truth that God can use both my light and my darkness. (2)

The very thought that God can use our darkness—that which we would reject in ourselves—is terribly exciting. It is redemption in action. The classic biblical example is Judas. Judas' dark side ushered him to the chief priests to betray Jesus. Judas' action was his choice, made in the darkness of disappointment over the kind of kingdom Jesus came to institute. However, God can redeem even the worst evil we can devise: Without Judas' betrayal, the Son of God would not have died as He did for our sins, nor would He have risen on the first Easter Sunday. No doubt God would have found another way to accomplish the feat of atonement, but the point is, *He chose this way,* using Judas' dark side for His ultimate exquisitely good purpose.

We must claim the monster. We must realize that Christ loves even the beast in us, and we cannot fully experience the waterfall of God's forgiveness and love unless we give all of ourselves to Him. This is the first step in accepting God's love for us—to love ourselves, just as we are.

The Need to Receive Love Before We Can Give It

The second interpretation of *Frankenstein* is that the monster cannot love himself or others until he's experienced love. Every time the monster meets Dr. Frankenstein, he receives further rejection, and the monster's two face-to-face encounters with other people—

both of whom he is trying to help—bring only revilement and disgust because he is so frightfully ugly. The monster thus knows nothing but rejection. This second interpretation of the story involves Dr. Frankenstein as a parent who created a monster because he failed to love his child.

One Saturday morning when my husband was a seminarian in Alexandria, Virginia, I took the Metro into Washington, D.C. to the central library. Unlike the usual weekday crush of hurried commuters, the yellow line station echoed with emptiness when I boarded at the Pentagon. Rows of vacant plastic chairs faced me until two scraggly-haired guys wearing torn jeans swaggered on, towing along a tousled, fresh-faced boy about three years old. I soon figured out that one of the young men was the child's father.

As the Metro car whizzed up out of the tunnel and sped over the Potomac River, the excited little boy peered out the windows, perched on his knees so he could see. The father told him to sit down, and he obeyed. In spite of the child's good behavior, the two guys started to abuse the child verbally, telling him how awful he was. The brief scene culminated when the father said, "If you move one muscle, I'm going to throw you in the closest trash can, because that's where you belong. You're a piece of trash!"

I debated whether to leave the security of my seat and go whisper in the child's ear that he was not a piece of trash, that he was a precious child of God. Instead, I chickened out, afraid of what two abusive male strangers might do to an interfering, skinny female in a deserted subway car. I sat, sickened, in my seat, as the little face trustingly believed his daddy, and I prayed God would find a way to overcome the hard words shaping the child's image of himself as a piece of trash.

This was a living example of Dr. Frankenstein in the process of forming a monster. What are the chances the little boy will grow up into a loving daddy? What are the chances the little boy will grow up to love himself?

God as the Original Source of Love

Frankenstein's monster made several mistakes as he sought love—mistakes we often make, especially when we find ourselves in the position of having been rejected or abused by a parent. We keep seeking after the parent, as if he or she were the source of love and affirmation, only to get kicked in the teeth over and over. We have nowhere else to turn as children, so it's only natural that the habit becomes entrenched in us as adults. Though we may know with our heads that a parent is not capable of loving us and blessing us, we have difficulty getting the message through to our hearts. As a result, we cannot stop trying to get the approval and affection we need from the most unlikely source. Even if we are able to understand at an inner level that a parent cannot give us the blessing we need, sometimes we transfer the need to another person—usually someone also incapable of fulfilling our desire.

Consider this example: Betty's mother died, leaving Betty with deep feelings of insecurity and lack of love. Unfortunately, when Betty became a mother, she transferred her mother-figure needs to her grown daughter, and began to seek from her daughter the original blessing she never received. Over time, the daughter became baffled and resentful: She was not capable or equipped to fulfill her mother's deep need, and she was also deprived of a mother because Betty was too needy herself to be a mother. She never realized that what she hankered for was something her daughter was not equipped to give her.

Another mistake Frankenstein's monster made was in thinking that he could be made whole by *anyone's* approval. We get stuck on the notion that a person or something in the material world—success, drugs, a spouse, etc.—will make us whole. The wounded soul becomes invested in something material, with the hope or expectation that the object of desire will repair internal damage, even if the object of desire is something good, like the love of another person.

False Sources of Love

As human beings, we seem to be driven to God as a last resort. We sit on this earth in a room full of toys, convinced that the answer lies in distractions offered by those amusing trinkets we can put our hands on. Perhaps our parents left us with a hole in our hearts where self-esteem ought to be. We are mistaken to try to fill the hole with love from a sick parent; we are equally mistaken to try to fill the hole with anything earthly. The hole is a God-shaped hole, and as St. Augustine observed, we will not stop yearning until it is filled with His love.

By now, we all know that drugs, alcohol, work, gambling, sex, and food do not make us feel good about ourselves. We are bottomless pits, driving ourselves deeper and deeper into destruction if we look to these things to gratify low self-esteem. However, those of us in the church should also be wary of thinking that church work, churchmanship, social work, and other worthy, God-related things give us the satisfaction and love only the presence of God can give.

For example, one of my favorite Sunday school teachers announced that he had begun to hanker after religious books, feeling satisfied and complete only when feeding off their insights. He had begun to shun his colleagues at work so he could cram his lunch hour with books on spirituality. He resented his family's intrusion into his studies on theology and wholeness. Finally, he knew he had a problem when, on a car trip by himself, he wedged a book inside the circle of his steering wheel and read the entire book while driving on the highway. He couldn't stop reading, even if it meant he died in a car crash.

The book was about the Christian life.

"What's wrong with this picture?" he asked the class.

After prayer and reflection, he realized his problem was a case of misplaced desire. Religious books made him feel good for awhile, but, oh, so quickly, the restlessness began again, the feeling of unworthiness. *If I just read one more, I'll be a better person and be more acceptable to God.* The hunger for healing sent him on a perpetual quest in the wrong direction. When he realized that what he really hungered for was the presence of God, not an author's second-hand account, he gave up all reading for Lent. Nothing, not even brilliant Christian insights, can take the place of God's presence inside of us, deep in the center of our being.

Like Frankenstein, if we try to fill that center with anything else, we will continue to starve for love.

Using Others to Fill Ourselves

Poor Frankenstein, externally hideous, desperate and craving inside. He was so hungry for affirmation—understandably, because he failed to receive it from his parent—that he tried to use people to satisfy his own needs. He was helpful in order to get people to like him. When we are not feeling loved, we often do the same thing.

Burnout and disillusionment in social work, or in church work, or in any of the helping professions, often occurs when we sign up for a job because of *our* needs, not the needs of those we are trying to serve. We become focused inward, not outward, and inevitably we become tired or irritated with the task. We are never appreciated properly because we are in it for ourselves, not for others. Janet worked at the soup kitchen because she needed to feel good about herself, to feel she was making a contribution to the needy. She burned out quickly, because instead of being grateful, many of the people were rude, angry, drunk, or mentally unstable. She had signed up for the job to help herself, not others.

It's almost a cliché to describe the insecure man who dates a stunning blonde, not to be in a mutual relationship, but for the way she makes him feel when she hangs on his arm, how she makes him seem more attractive in his own and others' eyes. A marriage made in hell is two people using each other for their own needs. Neither sees the splendor of the other.

Obviously, I am no psychologist. However, I would like to look at the development of personality from a metaphoric point of view. Our self-esteem is developed as layer after thin layer of transparencies is laid on top of the opaque projector of our inner selves. Before we know what's happening, we've collected several layers. "Honey, you are *so* adorable!" "Good job! I'm proud of you for working so hard." Or, "Stop that. Nice girls don't get angry." "You're nothing but a slob." "You are a piece of trash." Gradually a dominant shape of our self-image begins to shine through the layers until it is projected on the walls of the people around us.

Meanwhile, when we become adults, we try to reform what we don't like about our inner selves, adding our own images of what we want to become. One of the tasks in a healthy life is to revise the multi-layered image, to go through our past and delete the negative images, replacing them with images more healthy. Revision of the self is not an easy task.

In order for us to become integrated human beings, we must take a good, hard look at who we want to be. We must draw this image clearly, and draw it over and over. Then we must accept the other, layered picture shining on the wall, asking God's help in deleting the negative images as He reshapes us inside to conform to what He wants us to become.

Psychologist Dr. Kathryn Wortz describes the three-fold process of healing from childhood abuse. During the first stage, we have low self-images, but do not claim our victimhood. Trapped and ignorant of our dilemma, we feel shame and misery and experience low self-esteem. The second stage begins with enlightenment. We see that other alternatives exist, and we decide not to be enslaved, realizing that others have victimized us. We recognize that those who abused us are responsible for our condition, and we spend much energy in not allowing others to victimize us further. Third, we leave the whole issue of victimhood behind. We become whole, integrated people who accept ourselves. We become the people we want to be, the people God calls us to be, and we take responsibility for our own lives, forgiving as completely as possible those who got us into the mess. We walk away.

Avoiding Pitfalls

Disaster in interpersonal relations can come from several glitches in this process of self-determination and acceptance. The image we create of ourselves needs to be realistic. We need to include our flaws. We need to recognize what parts of the damaged self need to be healed because of abuse, and what parts are legitimate pieces of our personality and therefore need forgiveness. Excess shame is one thing, but sin is another. The person who has low self-esteem but who also cannot accept personal sin will be in delusion, and will probably be using other people as a projection for his or her own faults.

For example, this person may have trouble accepting responsibility for hurting other people. This person is, perhaps, a colleague who makes a mistake in calculation or judgment and allows someone else to take the rap. Or maybe this person is a marriage partner who is never wrong. This person can't afford a blemish on his or her image, even the self-image. A biblical example is Potiphar's wife. She lusts after Joseph, but when he won't respond to her advances, she accuses him, and he is the one who suffers in jail for her unwillingness to claim her own sin.

Closely aligned to this problem is the selfishness sometimes produced when we begin to heal and learn to refuse to allow others to "shame" us. On the whole, this is good. We begin to weed out the ugly, painful self-images among the transparencies, and we refuse to allow others to place harmful images on the stack. A person from an abusive background new to the process of healing is sometimes defensive and overly sensitive about being "co-dependent," going overboard to protect personal rights. I remember going through this stage, stalking every nuance of my relationships to make sure I always had the chance to stand up for myself. Dr. Pamela Howell describes a co-dependent person as the grocery store bagger who feels obligated to take your groceries all the way home for you, and put them on your shelves. The person recovering from co-dependency sometimes goes too far in the other direction, though, and refuses even to take the groceries to your car.

In interpersonal relations, we need to remember to honor the other person's image, as well as our own. For example, a young bride's mother and the groom's mother both selected a similar dress for the wedding. The bride and groom agreed to ask the groom's mother if she would mind choosing a different dress. The groom's mother said, "I'm not going to be co-dependent and allow my future daughter-in-law to run all over me the way *my* mother used to," and so she wore the original dress in spite of the couple's wishes. Freedom from codependency is not a license for selfishness. Perhaps it would have been kinder to respect the girl's wishes. It takes a person with strong self-esteem to take the backseat when it's appropriate.

Another difficulty arises when we realize that our problem with self-esteem is not our fault: A parent or another authority figure has created the negative images we are forced to live with. As we seek to heal from the damage done to us as helpless children, we realize we have been victims of abuse. Another trap is the deliciousness of being a victim. To realize our condition has been imposed on us at a vulnerable age is like being let out of a cage. We are freed from guilt when we can trace our shame back to somebody else's actions. It's not *our* fault! We were *helpless victims!*

Avoiding Victimhood

The great temptation is to linger in this guilt-free place, pointing the finger at the people who made us miserable. Because it is difficult to disown a sick parent, they often hang around causing trouble long into our adulthood; and sometimes the only defense we have against their barbs is to blame them and hide behind the shield of victimhood.

However, if we choose to stay as victims, we continue to stunt ourselves. We continue to participate in a sick game. For example, I know a woman whose alcoholic father had an obsession about her becoming a doctor, as he was. She became an accountant instead, refusing to live the life he'd planned out for her, and refusing to talk with him about the subject of work. He would punish her for being a bad daughter, claiming to his friends that she didn't love him, weeping at AA meetings because he couldn't manipulate her. For years she felt terrible, allowing herself to be victimized by this behavior. Then one Christmas, he sent everybody in her family a Christmas gift except her. As she pulled each present out of the big cardboard shipping box, she was stung when she reached the end and saw there was nothing for her.

Then she laughed. She saw through him, finally, and forgave him, feeling sorry for him for pulling such a childish stunt. For the first time, she was free of her own victimhood.

Healing our wounded inner child is a delicate process, and not performed alone. We cannot escape the web of our relationships. The more we love ourselves, the more potential we have to love our neighbors. The reverse is also true: The more we despise ourselves, the more likely we are to botch our relationships. The needier I am, the greater the chances are that I will use the people around me to fill my needs, rather than exploring them and loving them for who they are.

Any time we use another person as a looking glass instead of a window, we denigrate their personhood. We do not see them as God sees them, but we eye them for what they can do for us. Besides the fact that this technique doesn't work (even a hero's praise soon dims, and the familiar self-doubt creeps back in), using people avoids the real solution—accepting God's love.

Made in God's Image

The third interpretation of the story of *Frankenstein* involves seeing the relationship between the doctor and his monster as a skewed creator/creature connection. This interpretation points up the essential differences between the flawed, loveless doctor trying to imitate God, and the perfect, loving Creator who made us in His image.

Dr. Frankenstein created his monster by hit or miss, getting the proportions wrong, stumbling around in his secret study, not sure at all what he was doing. Our Creator, on the other hand, knows every cell in our bodies, every hair on our heads, and loves what He made. Psalm 139 says that God "didst form my inward parts, thou didst knit me together in my mother's womb." Our

Creator knew our bodies before we were born! Unlike Dr. Frankenstein, He knew exactly what He was doing when He formed each of us, and instead of spurning us, He was willing to die for us to prove how much He loved us.

While the monster is a tragic travesty of a human being, we on the other hand are made in God's image. We have been given the potential to be whole, sparkling people, and all we have to do is accept the gift. When we do, our lives start falling into place. We can begin to seek wholeness not from material things or earthly kinds of love, but from the Source of all love, and we can begin to mirror God's love to others. This process is the most exciting event in our lives. However, it doesn't happen overnight.

Learning to Accept God's Love

In fact, this journey toward deep acceptance of God's love reminds me of the Tibetan monks I saw on a television special, who were making a pilgrimage to a holy city. These monks traveled slowly. Painstakingly. They took two steps forward and one step back. Then they fell down on the ground, spread-eagle on their faces, only to pick themselves up and begin again. Two steps forward, one step back, then face down in the dirt. Over and over and over. Besides taking a long time, the process looked exhausting.

The spiritual process of learning to accept God's love takes time. To learn to love the part of ourselves we've been taught to despise; to learn to seek worth from God instead of from work, drugs, sex, other people; to learn to trust that the God of the universe *really does* know and care about the very cells of our bodies and all the tiny details of our lives—to learn all this takes a lifetime. But what better way do we have to spend it?

What does this spiritual process look like on a practical level? A character in P. D. James' murder mystery *The Black Tower* asks about the spiritual life: "Was it lived at the same time as the ordinary regulated life of getting up, meal times, school, holidays; or was it an existence on some other plane?" (20) To be effective, spiritual growth takes place in all the levels of our lives. A spiritual theory does no good unless it becomes laced with our feelings and behavior.

So here's how I approach the process. Once, as a young adult, I sailed into a large, exclusive cocktail party wearing a knee-length, green satin dress. Out of the two or three hundred women milling about, I was the only one in a dress above my ankles. I spent most of the party berating myself for walking in like a socially ignorant hick. Because I didn't accept that I'd made a simple mistake, I was totally self-absorbed, unable to think of anybody or anything but my social gaff. All evening, I played this tape: *I'm so stupid. I'm so embarrassed. Everybody thinks I'm a social retard. I'm so, so stupid.*

I was younger then, less confident socially or personally. The way I work myself out of self-denigration now is to replace the useless, destructive tape with a prayer. *Lord, I've made a mistake. I know You love me. Clothes do not really matter. Help me to focus on the people around me instead of myself.*

With this prayer, the spiritual life enters right into the party, and I end up carrying a little piece of the Holy Spirit around inside me instead of a cringing, insecure me beating myself up.

The spiritual life is not a fog, not a dream, not a feeling conjured up once a day during prayer time. The spiritual life and the love of God are knit right into the texture of our lives. A more profound example of the process of learning to accept God's love occurred during the seven-and-a-half years Stockton and I tried unsuccessfully to conceive a child. Because I did not sense God's love deep in the center of my being, every time I started my period, I felt unloved by God. Why else did He deny my request? I wasn't asking for anything He hadn't given all my friends. Even though I knew better with my mind, for two or three days each month, my spirit felt rejected. I would lie awake at night with tears in my ears; and I'm ashamed to say that it took me most of the seven-and-a-half years to feel, finally, that God did indeed love me. He simply had other plans—plans so wonderful that I couldn't even imagine them because I had enclosed myself so completely in the darkness of my despair.

God loves us. We must believe it. We must force ourselves to reach for the light.

God's Love Even When the Answer Is "No"

In the process of spiritual development, we are tempted to view prayers answered "yes" as an affirmation of God's love, not realizing that prayer is answered "yes," or "no," or "maybe," or "not yet," or with total silence—and that God loves us no matter what the answer is.

Especially when we pray for something that will make us feel better—for a job, for example, when we're out of work, or for healing, or for a spouse, or for a child—we rejoice when the request is granted. Along with the gift of the job or the spouse itself comes the additional gift, the assurance of God's love. We consider ourselves blessed. However, when we are praying deep in the night, wrestling with God's silence or with a flat out "no," we don't feel so blessed, or so loved.

Yet, having spent so many nights on my couch, I might argue that we are even more blessed than we realize. Because our need has not been met, because our request has been turned down, we are forced to dig deeper into ourselves and into our relationship with God to uncover the root of the problem. God teaches us the most powerful things through denial.

Conversely, when we finally understand what He is really after, we feel His love even more intensely. I have never felt more loved by God than when the social worker placed my children in my arms. "Oh, *this* is what you wanted for me!" What a fool I'd been.

Further, if God satisfied the craving of our souls with what we *think* we need, we would probably be satisfied quickly; not only would we be glutted, but we would continue to want more of the same thing. Both satiated and yet wanting more—we'd be in a contradictory situation, a double bind.

When I was young, a *Twilight Zone* episode caught my attention. A man died and went to a splendid place where his every wish was instantly gratified. At first he was thrilled, wondering how he had gotten into heaven after the selfish life he'd led. In this exotic place, he had only to ask for a million dollars, beautiful women, mansions, Rolls Royces, and all the wishes came true. After a few days, though, he became bored; then the boredom grew into glutted misery, and finally became anguish. At the end he screamed to his servant, "If this is heaven, I want to go to the other place!" His servant replied, "This *is* the other place."

This describes, of course, the human condition of sin. No matter how hard we pray, no matter how hard we try to satisfy the gnawing need to feel good about ourselves, nothing from the world will stop the hunger. What we are really yearning for is God Himself. We demand His gifts to satisfy our cravings. Yet, only His presence can do the trick.

God's love and presence fill our lives in the present with love and affirmation; in addition, His love also helps us to deal with and heal from painful memories that haunt us from the past.

❦

Where cross the crowded ways of life,
where sound the cries of race and clan,
above the noise of selfish strife,
we hear thy voice, O Son of Man.

In haunts of wretchedness and need,
on shadowed thresholds dark with fears,
from paths where hide the lures of greed,
we catch the vision of thy tears.

The cup of water given for thee
still holds the freshness of thy grace;
yet long these multitudes to see
the true compassion of thy face.

O Master, from the mountain side,
make haste to heal these hearts of pain;
among the restless throngs abide,
O tread the city's streets again;

till all the world shall learn thy love,
and follow where thy feet have trod;
till glorious from thy heaven above,
shall come the city of our God.

(THE HYMNAL 1982, #609, *by Frank Mason North*)

4

Looking Back

You never find yourself until you face the truth.
—Pearl Bailey

Bill nervously nibbled the salty-sweet peanuts, watching the earth disappear beneath a bank of cotton-candy clouds, pink in the sunset outside the plane's window. As the airplane lifted above the Austin Metro Area, Bill's eyes had sought out and locked onto the university's orange tower, lit in honor of the graduates. When the speck of orange finally disappeared in the twilight, he sighed and leaned back in his seat, dreading the summer ahead at his parents' Colorado cabin, a dream home tucked in a blue-spruce forest high on a mountain crag overlooking a view almost too stunning for a postcard.

Though he felt slightly queasy, he asked the attendant for some more peanuts. He needed something to do with his hands.

This summer was going to be different.

After the plane landed in Denver, his younger brother Al, still in high school, picked him up in the family four-by-four. He slapped Bill on the back and muttered, "Boy, you better wish you were in summer school in Timbuktu. We might as well put up a sign in the yard: 'Stay away. Marriage in Serious Trouble. Parents Trying to Bludgeon Each Other to Death.'"

Winding through the mountain road, climbing steadily higher, Al filled Bill in. Their father wanted a divorce, but their mother refused to file.

"Why doesn't Dad just file and get it over with?" asked Bill, already wishing he were hundreds of miles away back in Austin.

"Dad doesn't want to be the bad guy." Al shrugged. Bill knew what he meant. Their father was an elected politician and a church leader, and he didn't want to give the press any ammunition in what was already becoming a semi-public brawl.

"Mom's hanging in there. She doesn't want a divorce in the first place, and she sure isn't going to be the one to file."

Usually when he pulled into the sharply pine-scented drive, Bill felt like the summer haven was a foretaste of heaven. Not tonight. He heard stifled sobs from his parents' bedroom before they pushed in the heavy front door.

After Bill had been at home about a week, he had almost gotten used to his mother's low sighs, her Elavil-induced naps. His father drove into Denver daily, returning home with a false cheerfulness that made Bill want to smack him across his tight lips.

One night, his parents locked themselves in their bedroom and went at it. Later Bill told me, "My mom just sobbed and sobbed, and my dad never stopped talking. Like a buzz saw. I finally went to bed but I couldn't sleep. Then suddenly, I hear a crash and the door slams, and then my dad comes barging into my room, yanking his khaki's on with one hand. With the other, he throws a hunting knife in my lap.

"I'm still groggy, but Al's already catching *zzzz*'s on the top bunk. Dad's frantically buttoning his pants. 'Hide this from your mother. She tried to slit her wrists. Now she's run away, and I'm afraid she's going down to the roadside park to jump.'"

Bill continued, "So I'm sitting here in the dark, staring at the glint of light shining off this knife. I'm thinking, *What happened to our all–American family? Last summer we'd all posed, clustered on the front stoop of this very house, smiling for Dad's political ad like we were all happy as Howdy Doody. Now Mom's gone to jump off the cliff.*

"Takes me about a minute, then I think, *Maybe I ought to go try to help.* I'm still stuck on the fact that Mom's a fighter. No way she'd try to commit suicide. *What was going on?* I wake up my brother and leave the knife with him. I get in the Blazer—Dad's taken off on foot. Half-a-mile down the dirt road, I start getting frantic. The dark trees close in on the road, and I can't see for the clouds of dust and the spooky blackness. Finally, my headlights catch two figures hobbling along—my dad lifting my mom who's cut up and limping pretty badly.

"Six months later, my dad filed for divorce. I guess he finally realized if he wanted out, he had to do it himself."

Bill told me this story five years after it had happened. Yet he remembered details as if it were yesterday. When he talked, his hand gestures and the intensity of his voice conveyed the anger he still felt. Since then, he'd talked with his mother several times about that night. As he'd begun to suspect, his dad had been working on her for months, chipping away at her self-esteem.

"See," he told me, "if he could get Mom to commit suicide, then he'd be free of her and wouldn't have to file for divorce. Failure for the marriage wouldn't be his responsibility. People might even pity him. I don't know if he did it intentionally or not, but he just got out the old chisel and went to work on her will to live.

"And he almost succeeded." Bill clenched and unclenched his hands. "Then the decent part of my dad won out over the dirtbag part, and he rescued her."

As he talked, I worried about Bill. His parents had both survived the scandal, and both had remarried. Bill, though, seemed unable to grow past that night on the mountain.

Then, I ran into Bill at a conference, eighteen years after his parents' divorce. He volunteered, "You know, I finally got rid of the knife. Not the real knife, of course. I mean the anger. Last year, I had a spiritual adviser who walked with me in my mind down that dirt road from my parents' cabin to the highway, and helped me toss it over the side of the mountain. After that, I forgave my dad. Poor guy. Even though he's still in public office, I don't think he's at peace inside."

He paused and grinned. "But I am."

Memories that Punish

Bill's story is not the only one like it I have heard. Roving among the people we all mix with are those wounded by horror stories worse than this one. In fact, I have a few gems myself. However, Bill's story is remarkable because he was able to get beyond his past—he did not allow his memories to stunt his spiritual growth. Dealing with what others have done to us is essential to spiritual health. Memories can kill us as effectively as disease.

Other kinds of memories punish us, too, long after they should be put to rest—memories where we are the villain, and every remembrance washes us with fresh guilt. When I was nine years old, I inflicted a mean-spirited injury on another child. A girlfriend cheated on me during a game at school, and in retaliation I wrote the cruelest thing I've ever said to someone on the back of her school picture. Smitten with guilt, I apologized to her that night, but I still have moments when I cringe at my heartless and calculating behavior. This is not to mention my adult trespasses: Our pasts are often littered with actions we regret.

So why do we continue to stay in bondage to the past, reconstructing the same vivid scenes over and over and over? Where are all the pleasant memories in the middle of the night? Don't we want our own spiritual health? What's the matter with us?

Jacob's Past

Jacob's story sheds a great deal of light on how we can handle the sections of our past that give us pain. In his youth, when Jacob tricked and cheated his brother Esau out of both his birthright and his blessing, Esau, naturally angry, threatened to kill Jacob as soon as their father died. To save his life, Rebekah decided to send Jacob far away to her brother Laban, to find a wife. So Jacob left.

But not forever. After Jacob had married both Leah and Rachel and had sired many sons, one day he decided it was time to go home. Although he had some trouble getting free of Laban's household, he knew it was time to face his past. He knew he couldn't live on the run forever.

He also knew that his past, in the form of an angry Esau and an army of four hundred men, could kill him. Esau, too, had not forgotten. Esau had probably lain awake at night wrestling with his own memory of coming into the tent for his blessing, carrying his father's savory meat dish, only to find that Jacob had been there before him. The unresolved issue between the two brothers had grown in scope and intensity, and now threatened the destruction of many people not at all involved in the incident.

The night Jacob wrestled with God, his past stood lined up on the banks of the river ready to meet him the next day. Coming to terms with what he had done meant survival; failure to do so meant death—either his or his brother's, along with most of Jacob's household. At some level, Jacob must have known he'd been a rogue. As he wrestled those long hours in silence on the desert floor, perhaps he saw the situation from his brother's point of view. Perhaps he gained humility. Perhaps he felt sorry, especially because what he did was irretrievable. At any rate, the next morning he faced his brother courageously, with meek submission. He bowed before Esau seven times, alone.

Jacob was willing to look his past in the face, come what may. Fortunately, his brother Esau was also willing to face his past and receive his brother with an open mind, accepting Jacob's gesture of humility. Thus, the painful incident of the stolen blessing—stuck for many years in the craw of both brothers' memories—dissolved in one moment of reconciliation and forgiveness.

That moment would never have happened if Jacob had not turned around and headed home.

We cannot reconcile our past by running. We must be willing to take the risk of integrating painful memories into the person we are becoming. After all, the past shoves itself into our present whether we want it to or not. The harder we try not to remember something, the more those images chase us. It's like trying not to swallow—as soon as we try not to, the urge to swallow becomes overwhelming. All Esau had to do was picture Jacob's smirking face, and his blood rushed as heatedly as it did when he first caught Jacob slinking out of the tent. In one quick flash, the present can be ruined by something that happened ten, or twenty, or fifty years ago.

Going Backward to Go Forward

The person I present to the world is a struggling, but fairly intact woman tumbling down the road of mid-life. What you don't see at first glance is that, actually, I am the leader of an invisible chain gang: Behind me, chained to my ankles, I pull along several other Me's from my past—shadow selves who try to order me around periodically. I have integrated some of these characters nicely into my present person, and they follow along docily. However, some of them still rattle my chains and try to take over as line leader.

Regarding character development in fiction writing, one of my creative writing teachers, Robert Flynn, always said, "It's the character's past that makes the present important." Our past— what has happened to us and how we handle it—is who we are currently. When we give our lives to Jesus, we give Him the entire chain gang, knowing that, remarkably, He loves the whole motley crowd and will help us, if we let Him, learn to accept the unacceptable persons from our past.

Therefore, a spiritual journey includes going backward in order to go forward.

How we handle our past is as important, if not more so, than *what* actually happened. Some people have integrated wretched abuse, becoming healthy, loving people, while others become mired in relatively shallow potholes.

It's the *process* of healing that counts, along with our determination to ask for and receive God's grace. In John Milton's *Paradise Lost,* Satan is kicked out of heaven and lands in hell. He says farewell to the joyous fields where happiness dwells. He greets the horrors of hell. Then he thinks for a minute and decides to make the best of it: The mind is a place unto itself. Inside himself, he can turn a hell into heaven, and vice versa.

If Satan can attempt to make a heaven from hell in his own mind, so much more can we, who are not stuck in hell, and who have the power of God to help us turn a hellish past into a semblance of heaven. God yearns for our happiness and peace. He is ready to help us out of our messes; we are the ones who sit in our sinkholes and pout. Grace is infinite, a fact we tend to forget. Besides, Satan is in hell by choice because he rebelled.

The Past Is Not Set in Stone

I have been referring to the "past" as if it were a single lump of fragmented memories. I'm not sure this is the best image. Just as we each carry along several former selves, so we reconstruct several pasts as well, depending on our current needs. Revisionist history goes through this process on a cultural level, revising history in light of current events. On an individual, personal level, sometimes a particular scene from the past does become monolithic, a fixed monument in stone, just as our interpretation of a historical event becomes calcified in our collective memory. But it doesn't have to be this way. That same past scene can be reexamined, reinterpreted, depending on our current agenda and depending on how badly we desire to overcome its power.

For example, say, you remember one Fourth of July when you were twelve years old. You'd just moved to a new town, and you were at a preteen party with new friends you'd been trying to get to know for several months. Being cool was crucial. Then your mother arrives. When she sees you about to light a Roman candle, she screams, jerks you by the arm, and, as if you were three years old, drags you to the car in front of your new friends who laugh at you and don't invite you to another party for a long time. To top it off, on the way home, your mother refuses to explain her behavior.

As a result, you harbor anger and shame until you are twenty-five. You carry around an image of your young and vulnerable self, humiliated beyond words. Every time you remember this scene, you also feel a rather large pebble of anger at your mother.

Then, one day you are looking through an old photo album, and see a boy you don't recognize standing next to your mother as a girl. Tears come to her eyes when your mother looks at the picture. Turns out it's an uncle you never knew about. She worshiped him growing up, and has never been able to face his death: When he was twelve, a Roman candle exploded in his abdomen—when it was your mother's turn to light the candle.

Suddenly, the scene in front of your friends loses some of its granite quality. Your mother becomes less witch-like, and you change from the humiliated victim into a person willing and able to pat your mother on the back and say, "I'm sorry. I never knew." This former victim-self becomes integrated into your current person and no longer whines and gives you trouble.

This example highlights several important points. First, understanding *why* we are chained to certain memories can help us unlock their power.

Second, forgiveness is often the key to easing pain that keeps cropping up from the past.

Third, looking at the past from a point of view other than our own is often the key to forgiveness.

Fourth, we aren't stuck for life with painful memories.

Fifth, God's power can release us from even the most terrible past.

Because our pasts do not stay put behind us, but browbeat their way into the present dragging along all the old feelings, our spiritual journey needs to incorporate these bullies as they appear, fists raised to beat us up. Squaring off with those memories, looking at them differently, honestly, is the first step in helping to purge us of their toxic effect. Fortunately, the Holy Spirit is capable of healing even the deepest wounds. However, along with prayer, I would also recommend a trained guide of some sort—a spiritual director, a counselor, a confessor, a sponsor. Just as a surgeon knows how to excise a malignant tumor to keep the disease from spreading, so a trained helper can contain the damage done by the poison of a deeply imbedded memory. We can work on some aspects of our past alone, in prayer, and using our own skills, but sometimes a professional or a friend can move us past a place where we are stuck. And sometimes a memory is too deep or too painful to be accessed alone.

How to go about dealing with a painful past? How to incorporate memories in a spiritual journey?

Storing and Retrieving Information

When our son Jase was two, his aunt and uncle took him to see the traveling Dinosaur Dinamation display at the museum, a room filled with towering replicas of ancient reptiles, moving and growling in life-like imitation. That night, Jase lay in his crib, alone, talking to himself. "They aren't real. They can't hurt you. They aren't real. They can't hurt you," he repeated over and over. I tiptoed in and bent over the crib. "Are you all right, honey?" I asked. "Oh, yes. They won't hurt you," he replied, hugging his raggedy bear and sucking his thumb.

Jase had already learned a valuable technique for dispelling the power of frightening memories. The dinosaurs, a recent memory, scared him, so he extracted a more distant memory of a time his father or I had calmed him down on another occasion—and employed the same method to calm himself. His self-talk reduced his fear and finally put him to sleep. That night, Jase incorporated two memories—the now-unfrightening memory of the dinosaurs and the memory of being calmed down. He became a stronger, more resilient little human being for it. We can learn much from Jase about the power and positive use of self-talk and memories. But how does a memory gain power in the first place?

To begin with, we are machines more intricate than the most sophisticated information-gatherers scanning outer space. Through our senses, our bodies record and process more data than the Hubble telescope. We can compare our life journeys to these information-gatherers, continually pushing the envelope into unknown territory. As we forge into the unknown, we are recording sensory data faster than we can process it, and before we are old enough to talk, we have already developed a system for storing and retrieving what escapes us in the ever-vanishing millisecond of the present. In the mind of every normal two-year-old is a vast memory room, already labeled and functioning.

As we grow, some of the files begin to fade. Others are marked with red as being important, but none of the information ever really leaves the room. Since we can never grasp the future, and because the present is gone as soon as it arrives, we hurtle through time, *becoming our storage rooms.* With no memory, we would cease to exist. The crucial question becomes how to access and use our memory in order to become the people God would have us to be.

Early in life, we have learned to survive by developing work-able patterns of retrieving information from our memory rooms. We have also developed means of using the events of our lives to reinforce the images of ourselves imposed on us by parents and authority figures. These survival patterns stay with us into adult-hood, sometimes long after they are useful. Children often cannot control what happens to them. As adults, we cannot go back and change things; therefore, the only choice we have is to change the patterns of retrieval and how we use our memories.

Processing Painful Memories

Because our eyes, ears, and skin take in more information than we can process on the spot, the sorting and examination of events takes time—sometimes a few minutes, sometimes a few days, and sometimes a lifetime. The present passes into memory status almost instantly; and the faster we process the memories, the more we can savor the present instead of dwelling in the past.

The choice isn't whether or not to process our memories. We are human, not monkeys, and cannot escape the task. (I might argue that even laboratory rats process memories at a certain level. They are less likely to press the food bar if they've repeatedly been shocked simultaneously.) No, the choice is whether we sort and examine our past, gleaning health and meaning from the events of our lives, or whether we allow the past to rob us of the pleasures of the present.

What does the process look like? Dostoyevsky's masterpiece *Crime and Punishment* is a world-class example of the process of coming to terms with a memory. Raskolnikov commits a double murder, and we spend several hundred pages watching him sort through motives for his deed and its implications. In the end, he is converted to Christianity and turns himself in. In the Epilogue, Raskolnikov finds peace while he does time in a Siberian prison, providing a moving example of the redemption of Christ.

A contemporary close-to-real-life illustration might be easier for twentieth-century Americans to relate to. Say a friend of mine, Wanda, was driving down a busy street and her two children started to argue in the backseat, bickering over who got to hold the tape player. While the words of "This Little Light of Mine" bleat over the sound of children screaming, Wanda half-turns around to tell them to settle down, and just as she turns back around, a semi turns the corner right in front of her. Quickly, she swerves to miss getting creamed, but grazes the car passing her on the other side. The events have happened so fast that Wanda has not *thought* at all for the last ten seconds, but has merely responded with instinct and adrenaline. However, her mind has been snapping pictures and storing them for her to review that night out on the couch when she can't sleep because she is churning.

Most immediately, the insurance company demands an explanation and Wanda is eager to tell them that it wasn't her fault, but the fault of the truck who turned into her lane in front of her. She is afraid the insurance company won't believe her, and that her insurance rates will go up. She may even end up in court, a terrifying prospect. Accordingly, she scurries into the memory room to fetch those details quickly. She goes over and over what she is going to say to the insurance adjuster on the phone.

However, other things are at work in the "process of processing." Wanda's children have bickered their way through the past two weeks and have been driving her crazy fighting over who gets the front seat, who gets the bigger Twinkie, who gets to hold the TV remote control. Free-floating anger over the entire incident attaches itself to her children: If they hadn't been fighting, she would have been paying better attention to her driving. She goes over and over the scene inside the car, trying to work through the anger at her children.

Other factors enter in as well. Her husband sighs and doesn't yell at her, but Wanda knows they can't afford the deductible to have the car fixed. Guilt sets in, and she relives the moment when she first saw the truck. *If only I'd seen the truck earlier. If only I hadn't swerved so far.* Desperately, she tries to change the scene as it happened, but the more she replays it, the firmer her guilt becomes entrenched in her mind.

In addition, Wanda is sad because she's hit some poor old lady's ancient Cadillac. This lady is about ninety, scared to death, and trembling as the police officer helps her out of her car. Her car is not dented, but scratched, and needs a new paint job; however, the old lady is shattered by the experience, and Wanda feels deep regret at having caused such anguish to a doddering old lady.

Furthermore, Wanda's father always told her that she was a lousy driver and that she would grow up to be irresponsible. She remembers her father well, seated in the leather armchair with a pipe, coolly dismissing her. She staples this early memory onto the memory of the crash, and lays them both out in front of her when her dad calls to find out if anyone is hurt. All he has to say is, "Well, Wanda, I've always been afraid this would happen," and presto, she's got a whole series of scenes to relive, proving to herself that he was right. She *is* irresponsible. In fact, she's a failure. So she thumbs through the stack of memories several times, always ending on the moment of impact with the other car, and sinking into total failure as a person.

Finally, in spite of everything, Wanda is relieved. No one was injured. Her children cried because they were scared, and the old lady trembled, but nobody—not even the truck driver—was injured. She reviews the aftermath of the scene gratefully, sighing and finally dropping off to sleep.

Processing Memories with God's Help

So where is God in this systematizing, modifying, organizing process of creating meaning from the chaos of sensory data? Millions of people work through car wrecks and worse memories all the time without God.

If I'm going to take my faith seriously, I need to invite Him into the process. A spiritual journey is the habit of lugging every piece of wreckage from my life's collisions to the feet of His throne.

Several things to keep in mind. First, nothing that we have done is unredeemable. Even if Wanda had killed the old lady or her children, though God cannot bring them back, He can make her life worth living again. Look at Raskolnikov. Even we, who judge each other far more harshly than God, have pity for him by the end of the book. As for him, he is able to accept redemption and the love of a young woman who follows him to Siberia.

Memories give us trouble because they are superglued to emotions, and emotions know no tense but the present. So when we lift a memory to God and ask Him to help us work through it, we offer a present emotion clinging to a past event.

The sooner we work through the unpleasantness, the better. Memories get stuck in the "pending" file and continue to haunt us because we did not process them completely at an earlier stage.

Going back to the car wreck, let's take the emotions one by one and process the incident with the help of the Holy Spirit. First, hassles with insurance companies seem to breed nervousness and frustration. The insurance forms, the phone calls with adjusters daunt us; but besides the sheaves of paperwork, fear undergirds the endless blank spaces to fill out. *What if it's my fault? What if I have to go to court? What if the old lady sues me? What if my insurance rates go sky-high?* A little knot tends to form somewhere along the intestines as we contemplate the consequences of the collision.

God has given us many promises to allay our fears. Time and again the psalmist trembles with fear, but finds refuge in the Lord. Take Psalm 23: "Even though I walk through the valley of the shadow of death, I fear no evil; for thou art with me; thy rod and thy staff, they comfort me." We can claim this comfort as our own. Our job is to squeeze the truth as we perceive it into the little boxes on the form, and leave the consequences to God. If our insurance payments go up, God will help us find a way to meet them. If we have to go to court, God will be with us in the docket. Whatever we fear, God will help us work it out—if we will give the problem to Him instead of continuing to stew about it ourselves. Fill out those insurance forms, address the envelope, stamp it, and then mark it with the sign of the cross. When you mail it, get rid of it. It's God's problem once we let it go.

What about Wanda's anger at her children? If I'd been in this situation, first I'd pray for discernment to see what part is scapegoat anger and what part is righteous anger. Irritation at the incessant bickering of siblings is normal, but it is not okay to make them the scapegoats for the entire car wreck. Because I have a problem with anger (anger was not acceptable for me to express growing up), I would probably ask God to show me the best way to discipline the kids ("When you fight, I feel angry, especially when the fighting distracts my driving"). Then I would try to practice what I preach to my children; I'd pick an acceptable way to express my anger (talking it out with a friend, crying, hitting the pillow, scribbling the anger into a journal, etc.) and go for it. If I'm honest, I'd probably be angry at myself for not pulling over to handle the situation, and I'd probably have to pray for help in forgiving both the kids and myself.

The point, though, is to embrace the emotion, then to let it go. Over the years, unresolved anger gets hotter and hotter, simmering, then slowly roiling, finally reaching a full-fledged boil that continues to burn and destroy. Marriage and family therapist Jim May explains that this unresolved anger turns into resentment, which is expressed as rage.

Next, guilt. Even after she's apologized the first five or six times and her husband has accepted all the apologies, Wanda still feels guilty every time she drives past that intersection. Guilt is another emotion difficult to relinquish. But guilt is what the cross is all about. Yes, we mess up. Yes, we sin, causing damage in people's lives. The Good News is that Christ has borne all our sins—even car wrecks—on the cross, and we are forgiven. Our guilt was nailed right up there with Christ, and it's an insult to Him for us to cling to it as if it were a teddy bear. As Christians, we are *obligated* to give up guilt. Jesus—and husbands—don't want to hear "I'm so sorry" another time. They want us to get on with life. God wants us to relinquish that sick feeling of remorse, and let peace replace it in our hearts. Fortunately, we can pray to the Holy Spirit to help us to pry our sticky fingers away from our excess guilt and send it up to God along with the fear and the anger.

What about our sadness at the old lady's plight? Perhaps God can show us something to do to make her feel better. Maybe she'd like a visit at home. Maybe she'd like some flowers from the garden, or a loaf of bread. Again, God can lead us in overcoming this emotion.

Once I ran over a cat that darted out in front of my car. The cat's family witnessed the whole thing and realized there was nothing I could do, but the mother was devastated. An older neighbor came out to see what the problem was, and saw me trying vainly to comfort the family. Finally, I stood by the side of the road, paralyzed with remorse and sadness. After the family went inside, this older woman steered me into her living room and prayed with me. I can't even remember what she prayed, but she helped me overcome the sadness I felt. The very presence of God diluted the sadness and gave me comfort.

The relief Wanda feels is the easiest part of the memory. Gratefully, she thanks God that angels were, after all, hovering over her wheels. Remembering the bare whisper of the scrape against the old lady's Cadillac, knowing the sound could have been a blood-curdling scream and a crush of steel, sends her to her knees in gratitude.

Finally, though—and this takes the longest to work through— Wanda has to deal with the memory of her father as well as the memory of the crash: shame, failure. Working through old stuff can be excruciating; many of us have a backlog of memories like this, with few of them resolved. Although it's tempting to add this one to the stack, sooner or later, Wanda knows—as we all know—that she'll have to deal with the whole mess.

Deep Memories from Childhood

Dealing with childhood memories simply takes time. Like peeling an onion layer by layer, the process involves skill and can make us cry. I could devote an entire book to just this topic, but others have already done a much better job. *Healing of Memories* by David A. Seamands, for example, helped me when I dove into my past, determined to clear up some of those recurring joy-spoilers.

One thing I had to learn on my own the hard way, though, is that when painful memories surge inside us, the crucial questions to ask God are often painfully honest: *What prize am I getting by allowing myself to become embroiled in this memory? At some level do I enjoy being a victim? Do I gain power by recalling this miserable event? Do I need to punish myself? Does my anger give me energy? Is reliving my anger, fear, guilt easier than performing the more difficult task of forgiveness? Why am I unwilling to allow God to help me resolve this memory, to untangle the strands of emotions that choke me now, to smooth the broken relationship, to file the memory away peacefully?*

God can help us relinquish anything. So what do we get out of hogging the whole miserable experience to ourselves and repeating it over and over?

This is where another person comes in handy. A close friend or a spiritual adviser may be able to see something we are not willing to face about ourselves. An observer might notice, "You know, when you were a child and you found your mother drunk on the steps, your anger gave you the energy to survive. But now your mother's passed away. She's done all the damage to you that she can. You can stop being angry now. She can't hurt or disappoint you anymore."

If we look carefully and prayerfully at the reasons we nourish miserable memories, we may be very surprised. Speaking personally, my parents' divorce was more or less one-sided, and I have some painful memories of when my father left. I harbored these memories for years, allowing a single phone call to dredge them up, embarking on a three-day binge of painful recollection. Why? The divorce was final. Both parents eventually remarried, but I held tight to those memories. Why? Finally, I realized I wanted to punish my father by remaining angry at him. In a childish way, I thought that if I refused to let go of those memories, which by now had taken place many years ago—then he would somehow suffer as we had for what he had done.

I was mistaken. The only person who suffered was me. God finally got it through my thick head that forgiveness is more powerful than anger, and certainly easier on the digestive tract. It took years before I could look honestly at why I had given those past memories power to ruin my present. But God is gentle and patient, and His timing beats mine every time. He waited until I was ready to accept the unpleasant truth about myself, then He opened my eyes. Now, those memories have been flattened and pasted in the proper file, where they seldom trouble me.

Another thing I've learned on my couch thrashing out troublesome memories is to ask God if there's anything I can *do* to help reconcile the past. Tossing and turning in the dark, being whipped about by uncontrolled emotion is one thing. *Doing something about it* is another. Because forgiveness is so often the key to putting a painful memory to rest—either forgiving a person who hurts us, or forgiving ourselves—more often than not a phone call ultimately needs to be made, or a letter written, or some action taken indicating an attempt to patch things up. Twelve-step programs call it *making amends*.

After a number of years, I realized I had to do something to cement the healing of the memories surrounding my parents' divorce. As a result, I wrote my dad a letter—in pencil and smudged from erasures; nevertheless, I girded myself up and sent it. An action in the concrete world helps keep the memory from sliding back in, even after you think you've worked through everything. Perhaps, like Jacob's brother, the other person is just waiting for a chance at reconciliation. Maybe they've been troubled at night as well.

As I write this, I realize how easy this process sounds on paper. It is not. Years of angst have led to a plateau of a reconciliation of sorts, but it is a place that still quakes with tremors from underground sources.

A friend told me a moving story of her reconciliation with her abusive father on his deathbed. We were both in tears when she finished relating the total forgiveness that took place, and her father's acceptance of Christ. Stories like this are beautiful, inspiring miracles, but difficult for those of us still struggling at a lower level of forgiveness. The thing to keep in mind is that God loves us at whatever level we find ourselves—even if we are still in the pit, despising the very thought of forgiving someone who has wounded us.

Forgiving Ourselves

Self-forgiveness often requires an action too. Confession in front of another human being cleanses the soul. If the thought of a confessor is too intimidating, other actions can be helpful. I had a friend who had become attached to her own guilt over something, so she wrote out the incident on a piece of paper and burned it in her kitchen sink. As the smoke rose to God, she allowed Jesus to erase her guilt inside. Forgiveness wipes the slate clean, and, if you think about it, we are being disobedient and dishonorable when we harbor and savor our own guilt.

The Hospice Movement recognizes the power and the need for self-forgiveness. One of their pamphlets includes the following:

> Forgiveness is an act of the will . . . . Your healing will begin when you recognize that you are holding yourself in bondage to the past. You must decide: "I forgive myself the failures and injuries of the past and leave them behind me. I will not let the negative attitude I have absorbed be a hindrance any longer."
>
> In facing your self-guilt, you need to . . . . summon "the courage to be imperfect," as the psychiatrist Alfred Adler termed it. You must give yourself permission to be human, to make mistakes. . . .

The first step in taking action comes in asking God to nudge us in the proper direction. God's nudges sometimes come as whispers, sometimes as brilliant flashes of inspiration; or sometimes God burdens us with a heavy backpack we can't get rid of until we've done what He wants. In whatever manner He nudges us, we need to follow through. Ask my husband who put off a call to seminary for several months: God does not let up or let go until we do His will. Ironically, He prods us not only for the sake of the recipient of the letter or the phone call, but even more for our health and well-being. Frederick Buechner speaks of anger, but the same principle applies to unforgiveness. He speaks of licking our wounds, smacking our lips over our past grievances, savoring the pain we give in response as well as the pain we've received. This process is, in many ways, "a feast fit for a king. The chief drawback," he continues, "is that what you are wolfing down is yourself. The skeleton at the feast is you" (2).

We are not at peace until our painful memories have been resolved, and sometimes they are not resolved until we have taken some action to redeem the past.

Grace in Forgiveness

Forgiveness seems to be a key element in letting go of pain, especially pain from the past. I know this. You know this. We all know we would feel much better if we'd forgive the evil ones who injure us, and who walk away smiling. So why would I rather sometimes scrub toilets than forgive? Why do I resist forgiving people who've hurt me? Why do I resist forgiving myself? Why do I instead wallow in my pain?

Here is where grace takes over from human nature. Human nature tells us, "They deserve to be hated in return for what they did." Human nature says, "I deserve some self-righteous indignation here. The person who hurt me is scum in anybody's definition." Human nature says, "What they/I have done is too bad, beyond forgiveness."

We need divine grace to combat all these lies we tell ourselves.

Forgiveness in the Bible

Two biblical examples reveal the necessity for forgiveness, and how God's plan depends on it. Back to the story of Jacob and Esau. Jacob acted like a rat when he stole the blessing from Esau, and Esau knew it. Esau had had many years to let the kettle simmer, then boil over with his anger. And the Bible makes it clear that he was angry. He'd collected a personal army of four hundred men to help him get revenge.

What would have happened if Esau had not forgiven his brother? Jacob faced this army with the members of his household and a bunch of goats, not a military entourage. Esau and company could have slaughtered the lot of them by 9:15 in the morning, and gotten home in time for lunch. Esau would have wiped out the chosen people before they'd even gotten to Egypt much less gotten out—before they'd ever received the Ten Commandments, before they'd reached the Promised Land, before David had been born, and certainly before Christ had entered the world among them. The entire context of Jesus' life, death, and resurrection would have been demolished centuries before His birth.

In this sense, God's plan depended on Esau's being able to forgive his brother, and to put the painful memory to rest. Though God, in His omnipotence, would probably have come up with another plan, still the point is well-taken.

A second biblical example concerns self-forgiveness. Both Peter and Paul flubbed up big-time. How would you like to have denied Jesus three times, after you'd looked directly into His kind eyes and told Him you wouldn't? How would you like to have okayed the murder of one of Jesus' followers, standing by with a self-satisfied smirk, watching Stephen die as stones tore open his body?

I imagine both these men relived these scenes in the wee hours of the morning. Yet both overcame their feelings of guilt and regret and got on with the job of building the church. Where would the church have been if either Peter or Paul had not been able to forgive themselves and reconcile these memories? What if they had felt so unworthy of their assigned tasks that they hung back in shame? We must use them as examples: God has jobs for us to do too. In the writer Henri Nouwen's terms, we are all wounded healers, yes, but we cannot help heal others if we let our guilt incapacitate us.

Forgive and forget. Move on.

I need to mention one complicating factor in the healing of memories. Forgiving a person's past behavior is one thing. Many times the relationship is renewed, healed, and reconciliation replaces pain. However, in some cases, either because the damage has been too extensive or because the other person refuses to stop the destructive behavior, forgiveness of the past becomes an ongoing process. Forgiving people for what they've done becomes forgiving them for who they are.

One of my friends is devastated afresh at every family reunion by a vindictive older sister. Because of the long-term dynamics between the two of them, along with the sister's refusal to take responsibility for working through her own past, my friend says, "The only thing I can do is pray for protection when I go home, and keep my distance. I also pray for Sis, but from afar." My friend has forgiven her sister, but the relationship is still troublesome.

Sometimes, that's just the way it is, and that's okay.

Time, and a Larger Perspective

Nothing helps forgiveness like seeing the situation through the other person's eyes. If only we could "see the movie" of another's life, especially the hidden bruises suffered by those who in turn bruise us. Feeding our own pain instead of forgiving the person who hurt us is a form of judgment. We refuse to walk a mile in their shoes, self-righteously thinking our own point of view coincides with God's.

God knows the whole story. God knows that the woman spreading lies about the priest was locked in the closet as a child by her father—for not saying her prayers. God knows that the man who fires a subordinate out of meanness is so miserably eaten with hate and ambition for power that he will die of a heart attack before he's fifty.

Our inability to forgive is often based on partial knowledge. If we knew what God knows about each of us, we might have more compassion than anger. Instead of consecrating our best energies in hating people from our past, we probably ought to thank God for them. These people have snagged our attention, and because we can't get them out of our hearts, we eventually turn to the Source of kindness, and receive grace in overcoming the pain. The people who wound us have great power—either power to make us miserable, or power to bring us before the throne of God and ask for the shower of blessings He gives to those determined to overcome this kind of injury. Childhood memories have been embedded so deeply inside us that it can take years of God's grace to wash the hurt from our lives. But because we struggle so deeply, in turn we are deeply blessed by God's presence and grace.

Nothing we have done, and nothing someone else has done to us, is so terrible that God cannot ease our pain. Instant healings do occur, but most of the time spiritual healing takes place over time. What else do we have but time? Giving conscious attention to bringing a painful memory before God in prayer is worth spending time, especially if it is three A.M. and we can't sleep anyway. I have learned to lie back—and whisper the problem aloud to God—what happened, my frustrations at being unable to let go, the list of inevitably inadequate reasons why I'm unable to forgive the person who hurt me, how sick I am of this memory cropping up. Finally, I beg God in His mercy to help me get over it, to help me forgive somebody who looks to me like a blackguard, to help me have compassion for this person, to help me file this memory away and move on with His plans for my life.

Some of the lesser pain actually disappears overnight; however, some of the deeper pain takes another 5,999 nights on the couch to evaporate, ascending, finally, like incense toward heaven. However long the process takes, though, I do not have to wrestle with these memories alone. Even when the pain is like a stab wound, the Holy Spirit is with me, surrounding me with love and working His way inside the wound to help the process of healing. We are never alone. All we have to do is ask for God's presence, and He will be with us.

The best news about dealing with memories is that we are not stuck for life with people from our past vandalizing us over and over and over. Though the process may take a long time, because of the Holy Spirit, we *can* heal. God has given us memories to teach us. As toddlers, we learn quickly not to touch the hot stove again because we remember the searing pain on our little fingers. Memory is a gift, not a curse, and God has the power to turn our horrors into instruments of instruction. Though some memories will never be pleasant recollections, they can cease tormenting us.

If it is true that we become our storage rooms, if who we are today is shaped by what has happened to us and how we have processed those events, then the greatest miracle is Jesus' sacrifice on the cross, and greatest gift the Holy Spirit. We are no longer trapped in a little room with our unreconciled past, tormenting us in the night. As Wayne Barber says on the Precepts Ministries "Course on Romans" tape, you are not a product of the past; you are a product of the cross. Nothing is too awful for God to redeem.

But we do have to ask, and sometimes this takes great courage.

Forgiveness at the time of death complicates the process even more. In fact, chapter eight deals with the subject in greater detail.

In addition to helping us tangle with and defeat—or at least diminish—painful memories, God also helps us look ahead into the unknown of our lives.

Almighty and eternal God, so draw our hearts to you,
so guide our minds, so fill our imaginations, so control our wills,
that we may be wholly yours, utterly dedicated unto you; and then use us,
we pray, as you will, and always to your glory and the welfare of your
people; through our Lord and Savior Jesus Christ. Amen.

(THE BOOK OF COMMON PRAYER, *page 832–833*)

5

What Will Be . . .

Worry often gives a small thing a big shadow.
—SWEDISH PROVERB

Roger walks into work one Monday morning, tired and groggy from staying up to watch the late movie. Before he has a chance to hang up his coat, his boss calls him in and tells him in three terse sentences that his position is being terminated as of Friday. He feels as though a swarm of bees has stung his thoracic cavity. He barely notices his boss is explaining that the plunge in the oil industry is to blame, not his performance.

Roger politely shakes hands and leaves. He finds a bathroom on a different floor, where he sits in the corner stall a long time, staring at the black-and-white tile, hoping no one will recognize his shoes.

He took this job eleven years ago because it was safe, with a good retirement plan, health insurance, and opportunities for advancement. His father had been unemployed for long stretches when he was a child, and he vowed to avoid the anxiety, the fear, and humiliation forever associated with canned pork and beans served around a tight-lipped table.

One week later, he finds it strange to be at home during the day. It's too quiet, in spite of the TV. Refusing to be discouraged, Roger sits at the computer and reworks his résumé. He considers the fascinating things he's always wanted to do. Perhaps, after all, unemployment is a blessing in disguise.

That afternoon, Roger calculates his retirement, his savings, his investments; he cancels seven magazine subscriptions and an upcoming vacation; he decides to eat at home instead of going out. The bottom line is this: He has eight months before he is in trouble.

Before Roger knows it, the first month is gone. He has been industriously getting his résumé around, and has had two successful, though not job-producing, interviews. He has joked with his friends about being "in between opportunities," and every Sunday at church he has prayed for a job.

By the end of the second month, he is depressed. He has started praying daily for a job to turn up, wondering if God is not a little deaf. He has stopped seeing some of his friends because their concern is starting to feel a little like pity.

By the end of the third month, Roger is not sleeping. He stays up until three or four in the morning watching whatever is on the TV.

By the end of the fourth month, he is shouting at God. God has utterly abandoned him, his friends have abandoned him, and even the people on the streets eye him as if he were an outcast (or so he thinks). A sure job falls through, and he cries himself to sleep, something he hasn't done for twenty years. Two days later his car breaks down, costing one-third of a month's expenses to fix. That night, he opens his first can of pork and beans.

About this time his younger sister has a party and insists he come. Roger hates his sister's parties. She has weird friends. She works for the university's International Student Office, and she invites people with whom Roger has nothing in common.

He walks in late, on purpose. His sister introduces him to two Chinese medical students, a Middle Eastern business instructor, four or five of her co-workers, and a tall African seminarian whose face makes him almost shudder. As he shakes Roger's hand, it's all Roger can do to keep his eyes off the three-pronged scars reaching from his ears to his chin. As soon as he can, Roger finds his sister's husband and strikes up a conversation about something safe, like the stock market.

Later, Roger finds himself gravitating toward the dregs of the dip, listening in spite of himself to the black seminarian talking about his home country, Uganda. He is telling of his arrest and imprisonment there. Without faltering and without anger, he describes the torturers who raked his face with hot iron spears, trying to get him to disclose his family's whereabouts. When he refused, they put him in a large prison cell to be shot the next morning.

It is difficult to believe this story. It is difficult to believe that war-torn Africa has come into Roger's sister's living room and is sitting on her couch. Roger wonders what this man did to get arrested, when someone asks that very question.

With dignity and conviction, he says, "I went to church in spite of warnings."

Roger has lost interest in the dip. He has almost—but not quite—lost interest in his own sad plight.

The seminarian says that he escaped when one of the guards turned to relieve himself. He had nothing, after all, to lose by trying. On foot, he ran at night for the next two weeks across a country the size of Oklahoma, arriving finally at the border, starved, his feet swollen to twice their normal size and his face infected with long, mean streaks.

Roger twirls the corner of the damp napkin around his glass. Nobody speaks for a long minute. The seminarian continues, "So now I am here. I am safe, secure. I have my room and food and school paid for until next month. I have fifty dollars extra. After that," he shrugs as if to say, *Who knows?* "I never had it so good."

Thinking of his own circumstances, Roger can't resist asking, "Well, after December, do you have a job? Do you have a grant to continue school?"

The black man smiles peacefully. "No," he says. "I have, how do you say it, irons in the fire."

Roger says, "Doesn't it bother you not to know how you're going to eat?"

The seminarian shakes his head, and Roger wonders how someone who grew up without indoor plumbing has a better handle than he does on the important things in life. "It's a funny thing about Americans," he says. "The Commission on Ministry ask me, 'What are your goals for ten years from now?' I laugh. I cannot help myself. I say, 'I hope I am alive.' What else can I say? It is unbelievable, this obsession of Americans."

Roger blurts out, "But how can you live without planning? How can you stand not knowing what you will do after December?" He pauses, then pushes on uncontrollably. "I mean, how did you live for two weeks like that, trying to escape?" His answer has become crucial to Roger.

Once again the seminarian smiles, not broadly, but enough so that the scars on his cheeks move slightly. "By faith," he says. "I live by faith. Believe me, any other security is an illusion."

Borrowing Trouble

John Newton, author of "Amazing Grace" commented on the

nature of humans to borrow trouble, both from the past and from the future:

> I compare the troubles which we have to undergo in a year to a great bundle of sticks, far too large for us to lift. But God does not require us to carry the whole at once. He mercifully unties the bundle, and gives us first one stick, which we carry [today] and so on. This we might easily manage, but we choose to increase our troubles by carrying yesterday's stick over again today, and adding tomorrow's burden to our load, before we are required to bear it. (29)

Jesus also comments on borrowing trouble, telling His disciples, "Therefore I tell you, do not be anxious about your life, what you shall eat, nor about your body, what you shall put on. For life is more than food, and the body more than clothing" (Luke 12:22–23).

Why do we insist on carrying tomorrow's stick? Why do we continue to worry?

Our spiritual journeys are lived moment by moment, not day by day or even week by week. God doles out our existence to us one breath at a time. To trust in our own means of survival and security instead of in God Himself is to miss out on God's serendipitous moments and events He has planned for us.

We are conned—by advertising, by our needs, by our desire to play God in our own lives—into believing that planning is safety, that knowing the future is security. Twenty years ago before I knew better, I had a friend work up an astrological reading for my future. Now I realize why the Bible condemns this practice: It's too tempting to put our faith in a prediction instead of in God's love and in His providence. He has a plan for our lives, and He reveals it to us in His time, and only when He thinks we should know. To seek security in the future through any other means is idolatry.

A word of warning: Jesus didn't say "don't plan for the future;" rather He said, "Don't be anxious." There is a big difference between being responsible for ourselves and for our livelihood, and obsessing over what is to come. The seminarian lived from moment to moment in his escape, but he used his head. He avoided natural pitfalls, and he planned as best he could.

When my husband Stockton was in seminary, I remember paying bills, hunched over the makeshift desk in our bedroom. As usual, we were stretched thin at the end of the month, and I began to worry about how we were going to pay for Christmas. Then I began to worry about how we were going to pay for tuition next year. Then (and this is a true story, I'm embarrassed to admit), I began to worry seriously about how we would ever afford a college education for our two children.

Then I remembered that we had no children yet.

Talk about borrowing trouble! Why had I allowed myself to get bent out of shape over a distant event? This phenomenon—getting worked up over stuff twenty years down the road, or even next summer—is what Jesus warns us against.

However, He doesn't say to take the remaining fifty dollars in the checking account and buy a new hat, leaving no money to pay the water bill. Jesus takes care of us, true. But we also need to be responsible stewards of the resources He gives us.

From Present to Future: A Labyrinth

Looking ahead toward the future involves choices made in the present. One choice leads to one reality, while another choice leads to a different reality. If we blow our retirement at the horse races, we will probably live a different retirement lifestyle than if we make wise investments; and we may not get to be the traveling snowbirds we wanted to be if we've squandered our money.

However, God has arranged it so that if we trust Him, though the path we select may lead straight to bankruptcy, He can redeem in some way our poor planning—because, ultimately, if we are serious about a spiritual journey, all choices about the future lead to God, even though our circumstances may lead us to poverty. For instance, one of my wealthy acquaintances from college lost all her money and approached middle age living with her family in a crowded apartment. "I've never been so happy," she said.

The original labyrinth was a structure created in Crete by Daedalus, designed for confusion, causing the person wandering through to lose the way. At the center raged the Minotaur, a beast of destruction. In contrast, Grace Cathedral in San Francisco installed a *prayer labyrinth,* printed on a rug close to the entrance of the cathedral. As Grace Cathedral's labyrinth reflects, the purpose of the Christian labyrinthine journey is the opposite of the original labyrinth. Though life may present twists, turns, blind alleys, and blank walls, God walks with us as we feel our way along, shining His light ahead just far enough so we won't trip or get too discouraged. As we journey toward the center of our lives, we move not toward a mythical beast, but toward God Himself. Jorge Luis Borges, an atheist, makes the commentary in his short story, "The Garden of Forking Paths," that postmodern life holds nothing at the center, that all is confusion and bewilderment—not only in a labyrinth on the earth, but in a labyrinth in time.

Christianity counters this, of course. God is at the center of the universe, and at the center of our quest. Though we may feel as though we move through a labyrinth, we are being led by a power greater than ourselves. The solution to the original labyrinth was to walk through the maze using a string tied to the opening to avoid getting lost. In the Christian journey, the Holy Spirit is the string, guiding us through the confusing corridors of life.

Undergirding each of the choices we make in life, God is leading us. In our ignorance or in our false desires, we may make what we think is the "wrong" choice; however, because of God's redemption on the cross, there are no ultimate "wrong" choices. God redeems all our blunders, all our stupidity. The crucial choice is choosing God over not choosing God. Our job is to hold tight to the string.

Forks in the Road

A poem famous for dealing with the future is Robert Frost's "The Road Not Taken." In this poem, the narrator has stopped at a fork in the road, and has to decide which path to continue down. Both routes attract him, yet he knows that he cannot go down both paths at once. He makes a decision, comforted by the thought that he can, if necessary (though it's unlikely), return to the spot and retrace his steps to take the other path.

When we stand at a fork in the road—no matter how terrifying the choice seems to be—we do not stand alone. Unlike the two paths in Frost's poem, both of which were previously traveled by others, the paths in our lives are unique, created for us as we go. God clears the underbrush ahead and guides us down special paths beaten just for us through thickets of time and uncertainty. Even when we think we're "following in someone's footsteps," we're not, really. Each life plan is different, unique. When we panic, scared we have selected the wrong direction, He simply leads us by another route to the place He wants us to be. Route A becomes Route B, or Route C, or Route D because *God is both the Pathmaker and the Destination.*

The thing I keep trying to remember about giving the future over to God is that, like control, it belongs to Him anyway. Through blindness or selfishness, I can stumble around trying my best to ruin God's plan for my life, but as long as I am living in Him, the future takes care of itself, no matter what I do. If God is the Destination of our spiritual journey, then we are freed from the fear of making bad choices. The present moment is all that matters. The future snuggles right into the present, and gives us peace.

Worry

Worry is a habit, and just like any other habit cannot be gotten rid of by simply wishing it would go away. In *The Imitation of Christ,* Thomas a Kempis said, "Habit is overcome by habit" (273). The old habit of worry must be replaced by the new habit of trust. Here's another example from my own life, illustrating the habit of worry. As the time approached for Stockton to leave the law practice and go to Virginia, I began to worry. *Will we find renters for our house in Austin?* The very weekend we first advertised, a couple showed up and paid in advance. As soon as that problem had been resolved, I moved on to another worry: *Where will we live in Alexandria? How will we ever find an apartment?* In a few weeks, we received a brochure about seminary subsidized housing, and found a place to live. Instead of enjoying the peace of that resolution, I next worried about our financial security. *How will I ever find a job?* Then I found a great job on Capitol Hill.

All these needs were met a month before left Austin. God couldn't have paved the way more smoothly. But did I quit worrying? No. Though God had taken care of everything in advance, practically shouting at me from heaven, "Don't worry! I'm in charge here!" I began to worry whether the people in my new job would like me or not.

The habit of worry had become a petty martinet, drilling my anxieties, keeping them lined up in formation for battle with the future as the enemy. Why? How had this happened? Partially I blamed my personality. (I am a strong "J" on the Myers-Briggs personality test, a person who needs planning.) I also blamed an unsettled father with addictive tendencies who'd moved us almost every year during my formative adolescence. No wonder the future scared me! Then I recognized the truth: Worry is the skin rash of a deeper, systemic disease—a lack of trust in God. Worry is a faith issue, not an emotional or background issue. If the habit of worry had developed because of insecurity about life and what God's plan is, then worry would have to be overcome through better habits of spirituality and faith.

I wish I could say I have by now learned to trust completely, and that my life is like floating down the river of faith on an innertube with a soft drink in my hand and my feet propped up. I'm not quite there yet. But I'm better. Even in the midst of some crisis, I am now able to shelve the problem in God's closet faster than before. Just like any bad habit (smoking, biting fingernails, gossiping), the habit of worry can be overcome with discipline and prayer.

The first step is desire, wanting to change. The next step is recognition, catching that initial tightening around the chest, or the acid stomach. Our bodies clue us in to our problems faster than our brains, and this kind of stress is almost always accompanied by a physical sensation. For example, my heart starts to beat erratically, and I have to stop drinking all caffeine. My aunt used to scratch her wrist when she started to worry. Someone else I know becomes nauseated. At any rate, our bodies let us know when worry has settled in.

The next step is a barrage of prayer, because no amount of self-determination ("I *will* not worry, I *will* not worry, I *will* not worry") can stop the worrying habit. Going it alone on self-will only makes me feel guilty when the worry has dug an even deeper hole in the loose dirt of my peace of mind. Instead of this teeth-clenched obstinacy, I've found that a simple prayer such as "Jesus, help me trust You," repeated over and over soon focuses my mind on something besides the worry.

The next step is continued prayer, wherever I am—driving to the grocery store, on break at a committee meeting, at school. I pray for God to take the worry away. I picture myself curled up in the palm of God's hand. I pray for other thoughts—images of my children, a review of the latest movie, a list of things to buy at Wal-Mart, words to a favorite song—anything to replace the worry. Reading the psalms is especially helpful, the litany of how God redeemed His people, time and again, from the clutches of disaster. The Israelites offered praise to God because they saw how He took care of His own. These are words I need to hear when I'm in the throes of the drill sergeant called worry, who is trying to mobilize my fears.

Sooner or later I'm able to move on, confident that God can handle whatever it is better than I can. Though I still have a way to go on this one, just the progress I've made through God's grace in the last ten years—all the discipline and conscientious effort is worth it.

God really *does* take care of us.

How Jacob Handled the Future

What about Jacob? Clearly he was nervous about what he was soon to face. Jacob wasn't just worried. When his messengers reported that Esau had gathered an army against him, Jacob "was greatly afraid and distressed" (Genesis 32:7). "Greatly afraid" and "distressed" indicate more than a minor concern about what the future held for him and his household.

The first thing Jacob did was to make a plan. Like a good provider and responsible head of his household, he divided everyone into two companies, thinking that if one were destroyed, the other would escape. After Jacob had made his plan, then he prayed. Before God, he reviewed the situation as he saw it; then he asked for deliverance, reminding God of His promise to make his descendants numerous. After the prayer, he sent both companies and a gift for his brother on ahead. Now he was faced with the long, lonely night of worry.

As Jacob lay in the sandy desert floor watching the stars, what was he thinking? Before he knew what was happening, a man appeared out of nowhere, and engaged him body-and-soul in a wrestling match. In one sense this is the same wrestling match we are all engaged in on the eve of a big event that will determine the rest of our lives. The night before a child is born, the night before a job interview, the night before going on a trip, the night before saying good-bye, the night before meeting someone—sleep doesn't come easily. We seem to wrestle with God Himself over the outcome of the next morning's encounter. What will happen to us?

Jacob wrestled until dawn began to break over the desert sand. Though he must have been exhausted, Jacob refused to relinquish his hold in spite of the fact that God had said, "Let me go." Jacob demanded a blessing: "I will not let you go until you bless me" (Genesis 32:26). So God changed his name from Jacob to Israel, and blessed him.

This story suggests several important truths about wrestling with God over our futures. Jacob shows us that we need to make plans for our lives to the best of our ability. We are not to blow off our futures, lazing around, not participating in God's plan for us. We are to cooperate actively with God, sharing in the design of our lives.

Jacob also demonstrates the importance of prayer. Jacob's prayer is not merely a cry for help, but a long discussion with God about

His promises to Jacob. Jacob reviews the history of their relationship. Jacob's prayer is also specific. He tells God he is afraid Esau will slay the mothers and the children. Though we may not be facing something as dramatic as Jacob, still, prayer gives us courage to confront whatever's lined up for us across the river.

In addition, Jacob's story comforts us with permission to be afraid of what's to come. Jacob is human, and he is "distressed" with fear. He is no different from the rest of us. After he's done what he can, after he's prayed, he still grapples through a long night alone with God. Yet fear is not the last word. After the night of sweaty struggle, Jacob is blessed. Interestingly, he has to ask for the blessing; God does not offer it on His own. Jacob's nervy request, however, gives us permission to request a blessing from God after a long night of struggle.

I spent nights wrestling on the couch for six silent weeks after my husband's final interview with Holy Trinity, trying to predict whether the search committee from Midland would call us or not, trying to arrange the potential move's timing with my own job, trying to decide about what schools to put my children in. Six wasted weeks of anxiety-ridden sleep, nightgown wadded from tossing and turning.

Yet on nights such as these, when I have remembered to ask for a blessing, God has never failed me. He doesn't solve the problem instantly, nor does He send me a postcard with instructions for the future; but He's never failed to give me a nugget of peace, or a glimmer of a plan, or a shelf to place my worries on. Jacob's story tells us that we have the right to ask for a blessing.

Different Kinds of Futures

We have many different kinds of futures: the future we fantasize about, the future we dread, the future we avoid, the predictable rut future, the Surprise! future. Only two things can be said for sure about the future. The first is that it is fickle. Ask anybody who's won the lottery. Ask anybody who's had a surprise pregnancy. The mighty are fallen, and the lowly lifted up—in surprising ways.

Second, though fate may be fickle, God is not. God is constant, ready to hold our hands as we lurch, tiptoe, stride into uncertainty, and to hold us in His arms when disaster catches us off-guard, or to shield us when our expectations explode with good news. God is with us no matter what future we wake up in.

Dwelling on the future creates both problems and promises. As long as the future is the future, it remains out of reach. It's only as the future crests into the present that we have any real power over it, or that it has any real power over us. We give the future too much power when we project our current fears, hopes, and dreams into the abstraction of what's to come. Here and now is all we've got. But we cannot seem to resist the temptation to make real that which lies outside our grasp.

For instance, take the future we fantasize about. Fantasy in itself is a healthy psychological tool for all sorts of things. In fact, imaging is a constructive way to improve in sports. Remember the story of the man in a Vietnamese prison for seven years who improved his golf score by twenty points simply by walking the course daily in his fantasy? Picturing yourself receiving the Nobel Prize, or becoming vice president of the company, or hostessing the entire charity event is a good motivator for achievement. Fantasy spurs us on. Fantasy can help bring about desirable events in our lives.

On the other hand, spending too long in the movie hall of our dreams has a downside. If we fantasize too long about Mr. Right, for instance, we may be carving a statue in stone instead of in the clouds, and we may miss the man God is placing in our lives right now. The fantasy may become more real than reality, the future more present to us than the present.

The Future We Dread

Or take the future we dread. Suppose I fear losing my job. What are the consequences of this kind of dread? First, the present is ruined by bad feelings, which may or may not have any true grounding. Even if I know that cutbacks will be made next week, until I am handed the notice, *I may not be among those let go*—in which case, I will have tainted a large hunk of my present time with niggling and unnecessary worry. Unless I can do something about the situation, then dreading the future is not productive. Even if my fears come true, then and only then can I deal with the problem. Reliving the bad moment before it happens is a contradiction in terms, yet we do it all the time. If the event does come to pass, then God can guide us into what He would have us do next. In the Swiss psychologist Paul Tournier's terms, we cannot catch the next trapeze until we've let go of the one we're on.

Last summer, I was brought up short on dreading the future. One of my great fears is that something terrible will happen to my children, and as a result, I tend to be an over-protective mom. At Water Wonderland, I stood with my four-year-old daughter by my side, anxiously watching my son jump from a fifteen-foot cliff into the water. Right as he splashed safely into the pool, my daughter started to scream. I looked down, and her face was a bloody mass. Yelling at my son to meet us at the first aid station, I scooped up my child and ran for help. While calmly playing by my side, she had slipped and broken the bone beneath her nose, bashing her teeth in.

Here is the point. I cannot protect my children by myself. I'd been scared for my son, while my daughter played safely (so I thought), not *six inches* from my side. Yet she had slipped on the wet cement and literally broken her face. At that point, I realized the utter fruitlessness of dread; God alone can protect my children, and now whenever I start to worry about them, instead I give them to His care.

No amount of dread can either prevent or cause something to happen. Once I figured this out, the energy I used to expend in fearing for my children's safety, I now try to turn into praise for the giggling, brown-eyed, impish gifts God has given me today.

The Future We Try to Avoid

What about the future we try to avoid? This is the situation of a Jacob who might have chosen to linger, lurking the rest of his life with his father-in-law instead of bravely returning home to face his brother. When we avoid something we know we should do, we actually spend more miserable nights than if we gird up and just do the intimidating thing. Examples of avoiding the future range from the trivial to the sublime. When I was ten, I broke an expensive ashtray belonging to a friend of my parents. I spent a wretched afternoon, anticipating the moment the grownups would get back and I would have to tell them. I wanted to run away. When the adults finally returned, I decided to confess up front, and they were utterly gracious. I'd wasted the afternoon moping glumly, trying to figure out a way to avoid the encounter, instead of splashing in the river with the rest of the kids.

That's the trivial example. On a higher level, Jesus, too, tried to avoid His future. In Gethsemane, He prayed three times for the cup to pass from His lips. If there had been any other way to effect salvation, He would probably have welcomed the opportunity. Yet in that night of pain, He decided to embrace His future, the cross. He did not avoid it. Perhaps one night of wrestling with

His Father was enough. Like Jacob, He knew obedience ultimately costs less than stalling. The pain was over more quickly than if He had taken extra time to try to escape from what He knew needed to happen.

The decision to face unpleasantness is like lancing a boil instead of letting it fester. We often agonize and postpone for weeks over what finally takes only fifteen minutes. Jesus and Jacob give us the example of facing the worst, and prayer gives us the courage we lack to walk through whatever fiery furnace we think awaits us. The French call the decision to face the problem quickly *passer un sale quart d'heure,* translated idiomatically into "the bad fifteen minutes."

The Predictable Future

What about the predictable future, the future tedious to contemplate? I heard a sermon once on how to get out of a spiritual rut. When one day is much like the next and we hunger for variety, our lives can become stale, our relationship with God boring. At the time I heard the sermon, my life had been so topsy-turvy for so long that I turned to my friend and whispered, "I'd *kill* for a rut." However, the point of the sermon was well-taken: At some point in most of our lives, we look to the future and see the gray, dull mist of sameness. We yawn. We begin yearning after the ads for cruise ships. We get our hair chopped off in a new style. We paint our fingernails magenta. We grow a mustache. We open our prayers with a ho-hum feeling, and wonder if God isn't slowly putting us to sleep.

Our culture is not suited for waiting, or stillness. When our lives become "quiet" or "routine," our trained reaction is to seek stimulus, variety, noise, distraction. We look outside ourselves for entertainment, for novelty. What I've discovered in the few times

I've been granted a predictable rut is that the problem is inside myself. I am boring myself to death because I am not able to plow the rich fields inside. I have not developed the skills to meditate, to seek the small pleasures distinguishing one day from the next. People look alike; I do not notice a friend's new highlights in her hair; I do not rejoice fully in a parishioner's grandbaby with those tiny, miracle fingers and toes; I drive past lemonade stands, not stopping for the young, eager entrepreneurs in our neighborhood; I do not savor the garlic and the marjoram in the spaghetti sauce I've cooked a hundred times for my family. In times like these, when a predictable future seems to cast a pall over the present, I pray even harder for discernment: *Lead me, O Lord, out of this wilderness. Please help me to use this time to deepen our relationship. Let me rest in the unruffled waters of the present. Things aren't exciting right now. Help me to appreciate the simple joys I would otherwise bypass in my lust for more thrilling treasures. Show me the quieter side of Yourself. Help me to love peace instead of shunning it. Help me turn the boredom into something constructive.*

On the other hand, sometimes the predictable, plannable future is exactly what we seek. If we plan carefully and thoroughly enough, then we think we will be secure. The problem with this attitude (I know it well) is that we have planned ourselves a flat future. The bubbles have disappeared out of the champagne. We pay a price for safety in life. If we follow perfectly the itinerary of the trip, we miss out on the funny Italian vendor who sells us our favorite cerulean water pitcher. If we never vary our routine, we may not get caught in the rain with the person who eventually becomes a close friend.

Worse than missing out on some of life's richest experiences is that we mistake the security of our plans for the security of God's love. We have been in charge, not God. Because we trust in the false safety of our own providence, we lose out on knowing the deeper security of God's love. When I try to plan my future down to the tiniest detail, I picture myself falling asleep over my blotter-calendar, cramped and hunched awkwardly in the straight-backed chair, pencil clutched in hand when I could be enjoying deep sleep in a cozy bed with a good mattress and fluffy down comforters of the Lord's peace. "Resting in the Lord" involves relinquishing the pencil and walking away from the planning calendar, allowing ourselves the luxury of falling into the arms of God. As the *Episcopal Prayer Book* says, "For only in You can we live in safety."

The Surprise! Future

When we try to plan things ourselves, we may miss out on the biggest party of all, the Surprise! future. When I was fifteen, I had no idea I would marry the tall, cute boy who passed notes between my friend and me in English class: Surprise! During our courtship, I would never have guessed I'd be married to a priest instead of a lawyer: Surprise! During the heartache of seven-and-a-half years of infertility, I could never have predicted the staggering joy our two children have brought us: Surprise!

Many of God's surprises, such as marrying Stockton or receiving our children, dazzle so brightly we cannot see for awhile. We are giddy with happiness, speechless. Other surprises strike us differently. I certainly never would have lived five years in a place I swore I'd never come near: Surprise! The first year or so we lived in Houston, this surprise did not feel like one of God's delights.

The point of mentioning the Surprise! future at all is to underscore that God redeems even the nasty surprises. I had much to learn in Houston, things that I probably couldn't have learned anywhere else. By the time we left, I had made dear, life-long friends and had matured twenty years' worth in five. Now I thank

God for the "Houston experience" (though I'm not sure I want to repeat it).

The Surprise! future catches us off our guard. Sometimes we're thrilled, and sometimes we're wounded. Still, after we've gotten a Surprise!, nothing is the same. We're forced to reevaluate our expectations, we're forced to change our goals, and if we're lucky, we're forced into a more intimate relationship with the One who either engineers or allows the Surprise!

Our lives are like plotlines in a novel, with God as the Author. In literary terms, I have heard it said that there is no such thing as a Christian tragedy because, though tragic things may happen to the protagonist, the Christian always ends up in the arms of God. Death is not the last word. Disaster only brings the Christian closer to God. Nasty surprises or twists and turns of plot do not deter us from the path we tread. Because of the cross, we may march through earthly jungles, deserts, gardens, cities, but we are on a heavenly trek. No matter what our journeys lead us through, we always end up in God. From where we stand now, our future may look dreadful, exciting, boring, but we may rest assured that we are in better hands than our own if we simply give our future to Christ.

Blessings of the Future

Sometimes I think it might have been simpler if God had made us creatures who could not project into tomorrow, beings with no ability to see beyond today. I wonder if this consciousness came with the fall. Did Adam and Eve, scampering through the garden, ever give a thought to the next day—*before* they ate the apple? I wonder.

At any rate, we as humans are given this ability to project into the future, and we must learn to deal with it as God would have us. Seen in this light, the ability to project into the future is, in many ways, a gift. What blessings does God give us by allowing us to have this ability to imagine tomorrow?

When we feel stuck in a dark room of doubt, or pain, or discomfort, or angst, Satan sometimes tempts us to think we will be in this miserable place forever. Then God reminds us of tomorrow. The future is like a long, black corridor with light shining dimly under the door. Though we may feel alone, locked in one of the rooms off the hallway, we can hear the passing of feet, and we can pray to God to unlock the door and to walk with us toward the slim band of light visible just ahead. The ability to project past the present pain gives us hope and endurance, leading us toward the light of a better day.

Plus, our ability to see beyond our present circumstances gives us an appreciation of the present joys. Stockton's first assignment as a deacon out of seminary was in a dream church in Waco. We would lie in bed, holding hands, and comment to each other, "This is such a wonderful place! We can't count on being in such a great place forever. We'd better really appreciate our days here." As a result, our time in Waco was doubly special: rich in friendship, joy, and peace—and rich again because we savored each conversation, each worship service, each party, knowing we would not be there for long.

Theoretically, we should live all of life this way. We only go through once, and God gives us more people, more fun, more chances, more thoughts, more events each day than we can take in and appreciate. Knowing tomorrow may be taken from us, or may bring sorrow only enhances the good times.

A future gives us a cache for unmet present needs. If our present circumstances do not meet our needs, maybe tomorrow circumstances will change. If I am longing for a mate, or for a baby, or for a fulfilling job, or for a close friend, I can always pray that tomorrow will bring the fulfillment of my dream. In the meantime, God keeps me company today, helps me through my loneliness, and gives me hope.

Like the ability to glance backward over our shoulder, our ability to look ahead helps give meaning to lives that often look otherwise like an episode from the Keystone Cops. Looking ahead sharpens our focus, gives us direction, pulls together the past events and shapes them into purpose. No matter what we suffer through or delight in, when we look ahead, we can see God through the circumstances.

Gratitude

In the anonymous medieval play Everyman, God says of human beings: "They thank me not for the pleasure that I to them meant, nor yet for their being that I them have lent" (1641). Translated, this means that God is complaining of our attitude: We don't thank Him for the pleasures that He gives us, nor do we thank Him for our very lives, which He has loaned to us. Our pleasures, our worldly goods, our very existences are on loan from God. We forget to thank Him daily that we are alive.

I'd like to close this chapter with a story told by Steve Kinney, a priest in Fredericksburg, Texas, and a good friend. A man was on a journey from A to Z. Using road maps, charts, and the Mobil guide to sightseeing, he had moved from A to B to C to D. One day, he stopped at a truck stop for lunch, sitting next to a nice man who wanted to know all about his trip. The traveler said, "I'm on my way from A to Z."

The other man replied, "Oh, I know all about Z. I live there! Tell you what. Why don't you throw away all your charts and maps, and let me take you there?"

After a moment of consideration, the traveler agreed, and set out with his new friend and guide. The first place they went to was a party with a bunch of fun-loving people. The man had a wonderful time, and they stayed late. As they walked back to the stranger's truck, the traveler said, "That was great!"

Next, the pair stopped for pizza, lingering over the buffet and enjoying their Dr. Peppers. Then they stopped at a picturesque lake, where they fished until the sun went down.

The next day, they had a flat tire, but continued on for more adventures. After several days, the traveler said, "You know, I'm having a wonderful time. In fact, I can't remember when I've been so happy. But I don't see how we're making any progress toward Z."

The driver turned to him and said gently, "Don't you know? Haven't you realized it yet?"

The traveler looked puzzled and shook his head *no.*

"You're already there," said the man. "I *am* Z."

This story reminds us that in our spiritual lives, God is our future. We don't need to worry about our maps, our timetables, our plans, because if we are on the spiritual journey, we have already reached our goal—to live and be in Christ.

Direct us, O Lord, in all our doings with your most gracious favor, and
further us with your continual help; that in all our works begun, continued,
and ended in you, we may glorify your holy Name, and finally, by your
mercy, obtain everlasting life; through Jesus Christ our Lord. Amen

(THE BOOK OF COMMON PRAYER, *page 832*)

6

Dust and Wind:
Spiritual Beings in Physical Bodies

Grant us, Lord, not to be anxious about earthly things, but to love
things heavenly; and even now, while we are placed among things that
are passing away, to hold fast to those that shall endure. . . .
—THE BOOK OF COMMON PRAYER, *page 234*

*O*ur son *Jase has* always loved to sing. When he was a toddler, he
would sit back in his carseat and chime in lustily with the radio.
"You Won't Give Me 'Raisins,'" (which he substituted for
"Reasons,") was his favorite song. One night the two of us were
driving home singing at the top of our lungs, and he stopped
mid-phrase. "Mommy," he said after a long pause.

"What is it, Jase?" I asked, wondering what had caused such an
abrupt change in his mood.

"Mommy," he said soberly. "You can't see music."

He was right, of course. At under two years old, he had stumbled on a baffling truth for a little guy. How could music be so
much fun, so *important* to him, and you couldn't see it?

When I was seven, I remember thinking that every song on
the radio was played by a live band on location. When my Camp

Fire group toured the local radio station, I was disappointed to find only a room full of records and no stage with pianos and guitars and a hubbub of singers wearing tuxedos and sequins.

I also remember around age seven having a problem because I couldn't visualize the abstract concept of God. For me, to think of God as air or to picture heaven as clouds was unsatisfactory. Worse, even though Jesus was a person I could visualize, I didn't like the sappy picture of Jesus on the cover of one of our books of church music for children. Growing up in the 1950s in the heart of America (Norman, Oklahoma), I did not know a single male who wore sandals and a flowing robe, or wore his hair in soft, shoulder-length curls. The men in my parents' world wore burrs or clipped hair and liked football.

The soul was another problem. Desperate for a sensory image, I pictured my soul as a white, delicate, lacy pair of lung-sized wings resting lightly inside my chest. Somehow, when I breathed, God entered into my body. For years, I clung to that image.

Human nature has always been tempted toward images, lured toward the tangible because what we can grasp with our senses we can command, somehow. Plus, the physical gratifies more immediately than the spiritual. Take the golden calf in the desert, for example. Moses' abstract *Yahweh* confused the Israelites; they couldn't get a handle on the idea. Given the choice between a shining golden calf to dance around and a hazy, abstract notion of God, we are still more likely to pick the calf. God commanded us not to make graven images because He knows our inclination to select matter over spirit. Worshipping matter leads to death and decay; life thrives in the Spirit of the God we cannot see or measure with our senses.

On the other hand, we go too far in the opposite direction by denigrating matter and snobbily refusing to have truck with the body or with things of the earth. God created this world and everything in it—from amoebas to rubies—and pronounced it all good. The Christian challenge is to honor the dust of the earth, but focus on the life of the Spirit.

For medieval Christians, the difference between spirit and matter wasn't a problem because there wasn't a difference. All physical things were made from *prima materia,* or prime matter, which in turn preexisted in the mind of God. The idea of form, then, was a spiritual principle which infused itself into prime matter, thus creating the physical world. The cosmos, as the Middle Ages conceived of it, was based on Ptolomy's science and undergirded with theology. The nine heavens were a diagrammatic representation of the hierarchy of the spiritual realm. Dante's *Divine Comedy* is a literary illustration of both earthly reality and spiritual reality. Both realms were laid out in symbolic detail.

Since then, of course, science and theology have shattered Dante's (and Ptolomy's) views of cosmology. Yet today, for serious Christians on a spiritual journey, the relationship between spirit and matter still entrances and titillates us at the cosmic level. For example, our family recently "traveled" in an IMAX theater to the fiery surface of Mars, ogling at the technology that enabled us to move with the eye of the camera, riding over the orange-red mountains of this distant planet.

We were spellbound at the awesomeness of creation. Like young adults who finally appreciate the wisdom of their parents, the smarter we humans get, the smarter God gets: By the time we have figured out the proper instruments to explore it, we discover that God's creation is even more staggering than we thought. Space exploration reminds us of the cosmic dimensions of both spirit and matter.

More often, though, we work with the contest between spirit and matter at levels closer to home: the bodily level, the experiential level, and the cultural level.

Matter/Spirit at the Personal Level

First, at the level of our physical bodies, Christians—unlike many in this end-of-century climate of emptiness and despair—believe that we human beings are constructed so that we are capable of both spiritual and corporeal experience. We copulate, and we love. We eat, and we pray. We dance, and we yearn. Postmodernism claims that we've lost the center—we no longer have souls capable of receiving or feeling the presence of God. Although it sounds almost silly to have to reclaim this truth from an age eager to take it away, I repeat, Christians have always believed that human beings are built with both a spiritual and a physical dimension, a body interlaced with a soul in the mystery of life.

From the frivolous to the serious, several contemporary images for the mutuality and interdependence of body and spirit have occurred to me. Take salad dressing. As long as life shakes the bottle, the two primary elements are in a suspension. Once the body dies, the elements separate.

Or, take a person working a computer program. The computer feeds the data to the operator, who is the will, or the center of being who makes moral and spiritual choices. But it is the electricity, the spirit, which powers the whole operation.

Or, our bodies are like radios, and our spirits the waves; they work together to produce the sound. Whatever the process, our living bodies are mysterious mixtures of cells and souls, and Jesus died to save both.

The Hypostatic Union

In Christ, the tension between matter and spirit reached a balance never before or since perfected, in the hypostatic union of the flesh and the Holy Spirit. Jesus was fully human, yet fully divine. The rest of us are fully human, all right, but our spiritual capabilities are limited to glimpses, inklings of divine influence, and are also susceptible to the influence of spirits other than that of God.

The serious business of figuring out Jesus' Spirit/flesh ratio took the early church several centuries to work out. Early theologians excommunicated each other and many died trying to come to terms with how Jesus' existence was both spiritual and material. The Docetic heresy, the Gnostic heresy, the Arian heresy, the Nestorian heresy, and more—each emphasized one aspect at the expense of the other. The Nicene Creed finally worked it out: "True God from true God, begotten, not made, of one Being with the Father . . . he became incarnate from the Virgin Mary, and was made man."

Today, we don't burn people for heretical ideas. However, failure to address this question for ourselves can end up in another kind of corrosive death, like that of Robert Browning's bishop in his poem "The Bishop Orders His Tomb at St. Praxed's Church." This worldly bishop had competed for glory and power with his rival, Gandolph, for many years. On his deathbed, the bishop spends his dying moments not in spiritual contemplation, but in ordering a fabulous tomb, gold, ornately carved, inlaid with lapis lazuli—a tomb to out-glitter that of Gandolph. As the bishop lies dying, we see he has missed the point. He has mistaken the physical world of matter for the spiritual life. He has already died, long before.

I find our intricate duality fascinating. The spiritual quest braids body, spirit, and mind together; this intertwining is what not only separates us from our pets, but also, like a good guide rope, leads us to the spectacular vistas of God's kingdom within.

Put a simpler way, when we breathe in, God enters the lacy, embroidered wings of our soul.

The Spirituality of Illness

Perhaps the connection between spirit and body in the bodily realm is most obvious in sickness. A migraine, a pulled back muscle, dysentery, the flu—when the body sags, often the spirit sags as well. My particular bog of spiritual/physical depression is the stomach virus. On my fortieth birthday, I became deathly ill and lay moaning in my sister's living room. The spirituality of that experience can be summarized in a few brief words: "Oh, God, please let me die."

In studying that miserable afternoon, however, I unearthed several interesting insights into the spirit/body connection. When we are in excruciating pain, we are unable to connect with God in the same way as when we are comfortable. The cells of our body scream for attention and it is difficult to put away the distraction of pangs, throes, convulsions, cramps, and other aches to communicate in customary ways, either to God or to the people around us. This doesn't mean that we can't pray. It's just that the prayers are different, more immediate, more supplicating. When my body hurts, I don't have the attention or the energy to go over my prayer list, leisurely lifting up each person to God and singing songs of praise.

Because illness is a separate "place," as Swiss writer Paul Tournier calls it, we need to recognize and accept that the spirituality of sickness is different than the spirituality of wellness: It is an even greater opportunity for God to speak to us. I go to the couch in our den when I am sick in the night, and I have learned to lie back on the fluffed up pillows to listen to what God is telling me through my body.

Lying in my sister's living room that afternoon of my fortieth birthday, I heard God telling me some interesting things. The physical, "natural" explanation for my illness was simple. My daughter had thrown up two days before, and the virus had been transmitted from her to me as I took care of her. But she'd been sick many times and I did not contact the germs. Why had I gotten sick *this time?*

I lay on my sister's new gray carpet with my eyes closed, suffering, wondering what God was telling me. Most obviously, He was letting me know that, once again, I had overloaded my schedule and let my resistance run down. Sickness often carries the message: *System Overload.* More importantly, however—though I hated to admit it—God and I were having a power struggle. At forty, I had not accomplished many of the goals I had tucked away out of my own sight, but which had informed my behavior for several years leading up to my birthday. These hidden agendas came to light as failures, and it literally made me sick to recognize them as such.

Once God had shown me this crucial insight, I was able to wrench my life's agenda back from the talons of the tenacious, determined person inside myself, and give my life back to God. Under His plan and timetable, personal failures were not failures at all, but challenges I could continue to accept and learn from, or dismiss as no longer important.

If I had not gotten sick, I would have spent the afternoon at a party, and not done the serious spiritual searching I needed to do.

Sickness is a marvelous opportunity to deepen our awareness of what God is doing in our lives. We need to recognize that there are explainable and logical reasons for illness or injury, but if we will then open our spirits to deeper possibilities, God can tell us much. Perhaps back pain persists because we are carrying too heavy a burden. Bladder infections may indicate we are troubled by feelings we can't void properly. One spring, I pulled the muscles in my foot, and it hit me as I hobbled to class that what I really felt like inside was that I couldn't take one more step toward my degree program. My body had clued me in to a truth I had been unwilling to admit. Our spirits and our bodies work so closely in conjunction that illness may parallel a spiritual disturbance. If not, illness provides a break from routine, a time set apart to pray differently and more intensely.

Another spiritual insight I gained during the stint in my sister's living room was that we do not have a distant God who pities us from afar when we are ill. Rather, we have a God who's been there. Many times on my couch, as I have coughed and struggled for breath with a cold in the night or lain still as a rock so my digestion could recover, I have been greatly comforted to know that, on earth, Jesus also was most likely sick sometimes. Because He was fully human, I'll bet His body was not exempt from traveling flu germs or sprained ankles. To think we worship a God who has deigned to lie on a pallet in the middle of the night, in pain like the rest of us! What a magnificent gesture of compassion.

Our bodies, when we pay attention to their signals, work together with our spirits to deepen our lives in Christ.

Conversion as a Cellular Experience

The Christian journey, from conversion to death, is a bodily as well as a spiritual affair. At conversion, especially if it is a dramatic conversion, we may feel spiritually uplifted, lighter, joyous, and we may sense a change in our emotions; but conversion in two ways is also a cellular experience, especially in the long run.

In the Bible, the transfiguration foreshadows what happens at the resurrection. Jesus' body is transformed from the skin-and-bone figure the disciples were familiar with into a translucent, "shining" new body, recognizably like the old cellular structure. We are promised that when we die, our bodies will be resurrected in a new, splendid form. Included in the Apostles Creed is this statement of belief: "I believe in the resurrection of the body." When we make the decision to allow Jesus Christ to live in our hearts and to guide and direct our lives, we are not talking only about an ethereal magical wave of invisible air that washes through us, but a force that has the power to change our bodies when we die! We have access daily, hourly, to the greatest power in the universe, the force that can transform decay and, at a cellular level, create something new out of death.

We don't know how this process works, but the implications of the creed are clear. Our physicalness—that clump of cells we call our body—is important to God. He takes the physical matter of our lives and transmutes it into a spiritual, eternal mass of being when we die.

Conversion is not merely an emotional or intellectual decision, but a cellular one. A current theory exists in physics that the human body—indeed, the entire universe—is made of bits of energy bouncing off each other. Physics tells us that the underlying fabric of nature exists at the quantum level, a level smaller than atoms and molecules. At this level, the properties of matter and energy are interchangeable, and happiness and despair are not states of mind or states of soul, but rather electrical discharges. Studies in brain function have shown how we are controlled by the electrical discharges that jump the synapses and how "mental" health depends on chemical balance. The ramifications of these theories in the light of the conversion experience are exciting to ponder.

Scientists have long known that our cells are in a continuous process of dying and being reborn. Every seven years, we are completely new people, literally. The decision to accept Christ—like every other thought and decision we make—becomes an electrical discharge spreading like lightning throughout every cell in our body. Because God's love is a powerful but mysterious force for good, the impulses we are sending to our toes, our livers, our hearts, our brains actually form a healing charge, an electrical beam like a laser. The Holy Spirit, who participates in healing, has always been an invisible source of energy capable of performing all kinds of miracles, even at a sub-atomic level. When we invite Christ into our lives, the Holy Spirit enters our very cells. No wonder healing services are so powerful. Explained in terms of "electrical" energy, the Holy Spirit is capable literally of zapping the cells of death.

This is just about the limit of my understanding of physics and neuropsychology. This view of the body as an ever-changing force field of cellular energy dying and being reborn is not inconsistent with how the power of the Holy Spirit operates. Conversion is often a healing experience because new brain waves create new patterns of thinking, which in turn recharge life in our very cells.

Thus, Christianity is not just a good idea. It is new life at a sub-atomic level.

As we thrash out the issues of our lives in the night, our cells are also at work dealing with the pain we experience as emotion. When we are finally able to relinquish the problem to God, the release is emotional and spiritual, yes; but it is physical as well. Sleep comes hard some nights, but when we do let go, our bodies as well as our souls find relief.

Spirit and Matter in Daily Experience

If God as Spirit can enter our lives at a sub-atomic level, what about the grosser levels of experience we are more familiar with? When we watch TV, when we tend sick children, when we decide what job to take, when we plan family menus for the week, we are still creatures with spiritual capabilities caught in a material world.

A second front where we engage, coordinate, and integrate spirit and matter is our daily experience. In the last century, poet Gerard Manley Hopkins used the term "dappling" to describe how the divine enters our world. In this century, writer C. S. Lewis used the term "Godlight" to describe a similar phenomenon. Playing on both Hopkins' "dappling" and C. S. Lewis' shafts of "Godlight," I compare our walk through life to strolling through a forest, whose floor is brindled, delineated sharply between dark shade and patches of sunlight piercing through the thick branches. Sudden illumination of the soul slices through the darkness of material existence, brightening otherwise murky areas.

To put it more concretely, the Spirit of God penetrates the physical world through very ordinary objects—the familiar things around us we can touch, smell, see. This is the fundamental idea of the sacraments, ways God reaches out to us through our material world. The water of baptism and the bread and wine in the Eucharist become more than ordinary earthly water, bread, and wine in the context of the church service.

If we train ourselves, we can sense God's presence in every object or person we encounter during even a humdrum day; and recognizing the sparkle in the bubble is itself a way to worship the God who created bubbles and added sparkles for the fun of it.

An ideally God-dappled day would begin, as do other days, when the alarm clock unseats us from our dreams. Instead of groaning, sighing, lugging my creaking carcass from the cozy blankets, a more disciplined Christian might take the opportunity to thank God for a sense of hearing (unearthly as the alarm sounds, at least I can still hear it)—or to breathe deeply in the dark, wiggling my fingers and toes, letting my body tingle with the news that *I woke up. I have been granted another day.* The plunge of excitement I ought to feel daily should awaken my sloggy spirit, and should make me want to cry aloud with praise.

Instead, most days I stumble into the bathroom and stand like a mummy in the shower—where I usually miss another great moment of "Godlight." As the warm water slides off my chin and trickles down my back, I am reminded of God's love, how it slides and trickles all over us when we watch for it. I am also grateful on a more practical level for indoor plumbing. Many in the world do not have the luxury of cleansing themselves in a warm, steamy bathroom with sanitary water.

Once again, if I train myself, I can focus on God's gifts, of water, of warmth, of cleanliness, filling my spirit with gratitude instead of churning about how I'm going to make that meeting when I forgot about childcare. After all, we can't do anything about our problems at 6:30 A.M. in the shower anyway. We might as well allow the physical experience of bathing trigger an inner, spiritual sense of God's peace and presence.

Our days are overflowing with such moments. The smell of frying bacon. The pinprick mole on my daughter's peach-like cheek. My son's tousled hair when he wakes up. My husband's laughter. The sound of pecans dropping on the roof. Our cat's soft gray stripes. These are all physical things that trigger for me a spiritual experience—unless I am too busy and too preoccupied, and I walk past, seeing only the cheek, the hair, the fur, or hearing only the pecans, or smelling only the bacon.

Just like training for any sport, learning to feel beyond the physical takes discipline. I try to take inventory at the end of the day, asking God to penetrate my world, to make the ordinary gleam. With practice and conscious effort, we can all find God in the most surprising places: in patterns of tree bark, in sunsets reflected off skyscrapers, in the steam of hot amaretto coffee. The physical world becomes a gateway into another existence. Many years ago, when I studied at Oxford, coral roses near an iron gate blossomed as big as cabbages and became a divine inkling for me. Still, when I recall those amazing flowers, my spirit is transported beyond my living room, and I get a quick peek into another world, promised to us as paradise.

The postmodernists are simply, sadly mistaken. Human beings have not lost the capability of living two existences concurrently, with the grace of God: one, the physical body, cold and tired, trudging through the snow; the other, a soul rejoicing at a God who can blanket a field of dirt with such tranquility. The experience of transcendence eventually becomes more real, more important than the body, or the snow, or the blossoms.

Jacob Wrestling with a Material God

The story of Jacob wrestling in the desert enlightens several aspects of the spirit/matter dilemma. First, at the physical level, if we believe the story at all, we must believe that the struggle was a physical one between corporeal beings, not a metaphor for a mental, emotional, or spiritual encounter. Jacob, of course, was flesh and bone—*but so was the Being who engaged him.* God did not send a strong, allegorical wind to buffet Jacob around, but became flesh and blood in order to wrap His arms and legs around Jacob's. Jacob's entanglement with the living God was no spiritual, beatific vision like the ladder to heaven. If Jacob had any doubts about the physicality of the wrestling match, he was left with a permanent reminder: God altered the cells in Jacob's thigh so that forever after he walked with a limp.

No question about it. God met Jacob on a physical level. God, a spiritual Being, took on flesh for a night—to touch, to sweat with Jacob, to tense and flex real muscles so He could engage Jacob's total being. Yet Jacob realized the experience was more than a physical exercise. The next morning, Jacob didn't simply yawn and stretch, saying, "That sure was some workout!" No, he realized that the point of the encounter, though physical in nature, was spiritual in intent. He was girded with inner strength, able to face the task ahead of him.

Looking at the story on the experiential level, we see a new Jacob the next morning. Though he walked with a limp, he strode out in front of the company he'd previously sent ahead of him to act as a buffer between him and his angry brother.

What caused the change?

The day before Jacob wrestled with God, he'd prayed to God in terror once he'd encamped. He said, "Oh, God. You told me to go home. You told me You'd do me good, even though I know I'm not worthy of the love You've shown me. I'm only two companies, and I'm terrified that my brother is going to kill my wives and children" (paraphrased from Genesis 32:9–11).

Now here is the interesting part, quoted verbatim. Jacob continued talking to God, "But thou didst say, 'I will do you good, and make your descendants as the sand of the sea, which cannot be numbered for multitude" (Genesis 32:12). In his prayer, Jacob told God of the physical danger from his brother's army. Yet Jacob also reminded God of His promise to him, to spare him and give him many descendants.

This prayer reveals that Jacob was torn between a spiritual promise from God on the one hand, an intangible pledge from long ago that he can no longer wrap his hands around, and on the other hand, the clank of weapons he could hear right across the river. Which was more urgent, more powerful, more real to him that night? His actions tell us. He did not rest in God's promises but proceeded to protect himself from the physical, immediate danger. He gave his servants over five hundred-fifty goats, cows, camels, bulls, and asses as a present/bribe to Esau, and instructed them to go ahead to appease his brother. Then he took his family and sent them on ahead across the stream. Jacob planned to go last, hoping to save his skin.

However, that night, God came to him. Though we have no record of a conversation about Jacob's impending meeting with Esau, Jacob's behavior the next morning indicates a major change of some sort. The physical danger had shrunk in proportion to the power of God's spiritual promise to him. Because Jacob had grappled with God, he was given a blessing, along with the courage to march ahead of his two companies bowing down seven times before his brother's feet, by himself.

Interestingly, the outcome of the story reflects the power of the spiritual choice. When Esau glimpsed his brother, the physical danger vanished. Instead of attacking him, Esau ran to meet Jacob, hugging him, kissing him, and they both wept. I'm convinced this came about because Jacob believed in the power of God's spiritual promise over material evidence of the contrary.

Spirit vs. Matter: The Cultural War

God entered Jacob's spiritual existence through the physical world. And why not? Sometimes I think the medieval mind had a more profound grasp of important things than we do. We may know more about how the universe works, but both the ancients and the medievalists took it for granted that God could mingle spirit and matter in whatever way He wanted. Our culture today has a problem with this. In fact, the Christian battle against the culture on this issue is the most difficult arena because the war is so insidious. We are pummeled daily with hidden messages that subvert Christian spirituality.

Late twentieth-century America is materialistic not only because we desire more clothes, cars, gadgets than we need, swimming in a reality cluttered with things like a pool over-crowded with blow-up toys, but also because our culture—and not just the postmodernists—values matter over spirit. We love measurable data, from our caloric intake to the latest scientific discovery. In this climate, God's promises can seem ethereal, and therefore not as "real" as what we can see, hear, taste, or experience. Unfortunately, we tend to pick up the culture's yardsticks to measure success, even the "success" of our Christian lives, and often we feel like failures because we are using the wrong tools to gauge a relationship that cannot be determined except in non-quantifiable terms.

Travel with me for a moment, commuting from north Houston past downtown to the University of Houston, and I will point out along the way how our culture imbues its unsuspecting victims with its values. On the freeways of Houston, leaving at six in the morning, I have had plenty of time to study the claws of cultural influence.

The first thing I began to notice about the flying mass of steel and chrome on the road at dawn is how our cars represent us out on the road. Every day, I watched the race and the relationships between junkheaps, power vehicles, RV's, snooty cars, middle-class cars, low riders.

We drivers become our cars. To a lesser extent, every material object we own or put on our bodies makes a statement about us. We cannot buy a generic car. Even if we purchase a vanilla Chevrolet, we are saying something. We cannot put on clothes without sending out a signal.

The spiritually aware American soon finds that the myriad of decisions about our material possessions becomes a series of small skirmishes, mini-wrestling matches with temptation. I want a

Jaguar, but I want one for all the wrong reasons. So I buy a used minivan. (This decision is helped by the financial fact that I am a graduate student and my husband is a mission priest, and the choice is between a Jaguar or food.)

At every turn, we are faced with the spirituality of material things. Questions to ask in prayer include, *How invested am I in my possessions? Why is it important to drive an expensive car? Do I become a better person because of the clothes I wear? Why do I look to possessions instead of to God to make me feel okay? Do my possessions give me the security that I lack among the "right" people? Why do I consider some people "right"?*

In spite of what our culture tells us, a house is shelter. Clothes keep us warm and protected. A car is transportation. Period. We are not our possessions, but our material things reveal where our hearts lie. Serious Christians need to consider what we are saying with our toys. No wonder Francis of Assisi dropped his inheritance (and his clothes) in the middle of the square and walked into his new life buck naked. Having no possessions at all certainly simplified his spiritual life. For those of us who cannot give everything away, the sorting of belongings is a prayerful task.

The Insidious Power of Ads

Next, as I battled the Houston freeways south in my used minivan, I noticed the effect that tons of metal skimming by each other at high speeds had on me. Physically, my neck muscles tensed, my knuckles became white knots on the steering wheel, and my head began to pulsate in an arc from the nape of my neck to my eyebrows. Spiritually, I was a wad of angry, crumpled prayers. People shot the finger at me, cut in front of me, braked suddenly; and one man in a car next to me exposed himself. Although I counted my blessings that nobody ever pulled out a shotgun and blasted my tires or windows—which was not uncommon on the Houston highways—still, traveling to school was a daily adventure in the spiritual discipline of remaining calm.

Two things helped keep my total being from turning into a cluster of tight, sore sinews, directed within from a spirituality the size of a shrunken peanut: my tape deck and the Christian radio station. Some of the talk shows soothed my nerves and gave me a spiritual kernel to gnaw on as I negotiated among the other stressed-out people gunning their machines to work. When the talk shows got too emotional or pulpit-pounding, I simply turned on the tape deck to a variety of calm music and let it waft in and out of me as I breathed. By the grace of God, I made it through four-and-a-half years of Houston freeway traffic without either a wreck or a nervous breakdown.

The primary barrage of anti-spiritual, or spiritually damaging cultural messages, though, is the assault of advertising on the eyes and ears, through billboards and through radio. What I learned to do as I drove through the litter of billboards telling me what kind of person I should be is to diffuse the power of the ads by analyzing them, putting myself in the position of the campaign manager. Why would I pick that particular girl—is there a come-on in her smile? Does she look like the girl next door? What sub-liminal message am I trying to send to get people to buy my product? Once I had gotten under the skin of the ad, then I could peel away its power.

Take something as simple and benign as hamburgers. I passed six sets of golden arches from my house to school, some which had a simple sign saying "_____ billion burgers sold!" As advertising goes, this is pretty innocuous. This fast-food chain is simply saying that if you dare to dislike our hamburgers, you are going against the grain of several *billion* people, and that means you must be an insignificant person. The evidence is over-whelming. Unless you join this obviously dominant movement, you are nobody.

In God's eyes, of course, this message is incorrect. God loves every hair on your head, even though billions of people may be eating the same brand of hamburgers and you aren't.

I also passed at least one popular toy store. The store's name itself is worth considering. Who is "Us"? Why has this store so totally identified itself with its merchandise? The name of the store does not imply "We Sell Toys" but rather We *Are* Toys. This chain's unwritten message is that because they are so totally iden-tified with toys, no other store can surpass them.

However, this name also reflects the nationwide phenomenon of becoming what we do, of confusing our "being" with our "doing." For example, when people ask me what I do, I prefer to respond with "I teach" or "I write," statements that reflect profes-sional activities outside my essential identity. Saying "I am a teacher" or "I am a writer" are statements that subtly merge *who I am* with *what I do*. I am a child of God first, and I write and teach on the side. This is an important distinction for a work addict. Such subliminal messages as the name of a toy store invite us to participate in the process of becoming our possessions, beginning in childhood.

Another example is particularly powerful because it was a Christmas ad for alcohol. In bold letters, "_ingle _ells" shouted at the passing motorists. Fine print at the bottom informed us something to the effect that it just wasn't Christmas without the J & B. At first, I thought, *What a linguistically clever ad!* Then I realized I'd been sucked in. The profound, disturbing cultural foundation of this ad is that for too many Americans, J & B is not what's missing from Christmas—Jesus is. This ad tells us that Christmas is about drinking at parties, or that a glass of

Scotch gets rid of the loneliness that sometimes creeps in at Christmastime. This ad encourages us to seek salvation in a bottle. The messages here are not even subliminal.

Other ads are even bolder: "Celestial Seasons teas satisfy the soul," or "Play this week's lottery. Forty million dollars is a lot of peace of mind." Advertising like this openly acknowledges our deep spiritual needs ("satisfy the soul," "obtain peace of mind"), but suggests that the inner ache can be cured with tea or money.

Ads can be spiritually dangerous, full of false promises for happiness from things bought to satisfy our senses; and more importantly, they imply that when our physical needs are fulfilled, then our inner needs for self-worth, for love, for affection, will also be met. The array of products peddled from billboards, TV screens, magazine pages, and radios, are guaranteed in one way or another to make us deeply happy. We don't have to worry about spiritual hunger when we eat the right brand of low-fat frozen food: We look good, we feel good, people like us, and nothing else matters.

Advertising the Christian Life

I thought it would be interesting to look at American advertising in light of the beatitudes. American products claim, openly or covertly, a variety of miracles for those who purchase their goods. Buy aspirin and get rid of pain. Buy weight-loss products and get good looks. Buy certain cars and get a new self-image (tough-guy, sleek woman, versatile housewife, sporty-but-sensitive man, wealthy, effete, and so forth). Buy deodorant or jeans or perfume and get sex appeal. Buy beverages and get friends, popularity. The ideal American life as portrayed in our ads is a pain-free existence with the self-image of our choice, emphasizing sex appeal, youth, and popularity—all based on the physical world, and all obtained from products which can be bought with money.

What about the spiritual life? If Jesus were on TV today advertising what He has to offer, what would a commercial for the ideal spiritual life be like? According to Luke 6, Jesus promotes the following characteristics: poverty, hunger, weeping, being hated. Matthew 5 continues the list: mourning, meekness, mercy, pureness in heart, peacemaking, being persecuted.

Can you imagine how an ad for these qualities would run? What Jesus wants of us is not the American dream.

Besides the messages ads send to us, there is another major difference between the way cultural messages work and the way the gospel works. Any ad has two jobs to do in thirty seconds or less. First, it has to get our attention. Then it has to convert us. The message has to anchor quickly deep in our bed of desires and manipulate us without our awareness. Once we are on to what the ad is doing, it loses its subliminal appeal.

The gospel works the opposite way. Oh, the beatitudes get our attention quickly, all right, but then they demand that we dig deeply, examining our inner lives in order to understand their layers of truth. Rather than offering quick fixes as ads do, the beatitudes are, as A. N. Wilson describes them in an interview with Rosemary Harthill, "a series of endlessly frightening, disturbing questions about us as human beings, at the deepest psychological level" (110). Rather than settling for sensory satisfaction, the Sermon on the Mount demands that we bring our physical needs into the spiritual realm and let God reconcile the two conflicting parts of our natures.

We wonder why we struggle spiritually. We are pummeled, blasted, inveigled daily with messages telling us to go after values diametrically opposed to the values we should be seeking. The cultural messages infiltrate every corner of our lives, especially when we are unaware of how they operate. "Be successful. Show off your wealth. Pain can, and should, be avoided. You're nothing if you aren't beautiful. If you've got it, flaunt it." God's message seems ridiculous and impossible in comparison. Who would admit preferring poverty over wealth? Who wants to be hated? Who would choose to be meek, or mournful, or persecuted in a culture that despises these qualities?

In fact, what ad company would ever take on such an impossible product as Christianity?

The church! We Christians should be walking advertisements for these very qualities, and that is why it is so essential for us to address our spirituality: Our inner values seep out with every remark we make.

Knowing we are at war with our culture helps define us. In this era, unlike the first century, we are not thrown to beasts, but sometimes I hear lionish growls from people working heatedly against Christianity. One of my professors, a self-proclaimed atheist, used to bang the table and snarl with each new Victorian author we studied, "Take note—there were *no Christian writers in the nineteenth century!*" His anti-Christian vehemence reminded me of Hazel Motes in Flannery O'Connor's novel *Wise Blood*, a man who preached the Church Without Christ with a passion so intense that he was, in fact, Christ-haunted.

In a country hostile to Christianity, wearing a cross is not merely a fashion statement; it is an advertisement for countercultural values.

Too Many Bodies in a Crowded Space

We have now been traveling on the Houston freeways for a long time, and we are almost to the university. I have to make a quick stop at a local grocery store and get a cup of coffee and a donut before meeting one of my professors for a conference before class. A wreck on I-45 has set me back twenty minutes, but my stomach is growling. I grab a chocolate cake donut, glazed, and a cup of coffee, and quickly join the "ten items or less" line.

The man ahead of me changes his mind on an item the clerk has already rung up. I tap my foot, the pressure building. The professor I'm meeting is always prompt and will treat me frostily if I'm late. Looking around, I notice that the woman ahead of me has at least twenty-five items in her grocery cart. *Twenty-five!* Suddenly, I am angry. *How dare she!* When it's her turn, this woman chats about her pet schnauzer, leisurely unloading her cart on the black conveyor belt as if she can't even count to ten, and the clerk collaborates with her, ignoring the illegal array of items.

I glare at the woman. By now I have exactly seven minutes to get to my appointment, and it will take me that long to find a parking place.

This little scenario highlights several points about trying to integrate physical demands and a spiritual life in American culture. First, time in the physical world—*chronos*—is measured and partitioned into segments and it moves beneath our feet as surely as the conveyor belt at the grocery store. Time in the physical world is measured by consensus, and our culture values people who honor the common agreement. The person successful in our culture learns early to march to the beat of time, and not to float through a weightless atmosphere as if deadlines didn't matter. (In other cultures, such as the Latin American culture, time is not as demanding as the master with a whip, but rather a friend gently urging life onward.) Here, though, if we dare to be late—especially in professional situations—we need a good excuse. Those in power often use time to control people. Some doctors—not all, of course—are notorious for keeping patients waiting, as if time weren't important for those they serve. The tyranny of time gives people in high-paced jobs or those forced to wait ulcers and heart-attacks. Rare is the person willing to pay the consequences for living instead in *kairos*—God's time.

Because we are trapped in this temporal dimension, our spiritual lives exist like the two liquids in a lava lamp—one kind of time suspended and yet moving within another. The difficult part is how to "squeeze" *kairos* into a tightly packed *chronos* schedule. Having a scheduled quiet time is one way. In a truly integrated spiritual life, the dilemma at the grocery store is how to find inner peace when time is squeezing you.

Prayer, of course, works well as a silent removal of our attention away from the frustrating circumstances and onto the Lord. Sometimes I simply tell Him how frustrated I am, in this particular case how I made a bad decision to stop and get a donut, but that it still didn't seem fair that the woman with the twenty-five items hogged in line. Then I ask forgiveness for my angry feelings for her. Pretty soon, I'm back in my car, praying for the old cliché—a parking spot.

The second point the scenario suggests is the effect of so many anonymous bodies all trying to get their needs met. In a small town, I might have known the woman, and could have talked with her. She would have been Bessie Smith who lives next door to Aunt Louise, and I could have said, "I'm in a terrible rush. Do you mind if I go ahead of you?" Or, I could have teased her about whether she could count. Instead, we live in a culture of foreign bodies brushing up against each other, and the souls within are lost. Every day we read about people who kill each other over more trivial things than getting in the wrong line.

Third is this trivialization of our culture. It's far easier to become enraged over a woman trying to cheat by sneaking twenty-five items through the ten-item line than it is to become upset about, say, world hunger or injustice. Our attention is continually grabbed by the minutia of our lives. Even the choice of donuts (chocolate, cake, glazed, sprinkled, blueberry, long johns, bear claws, etc., etc., etc.) becomes a big event. Just to get through the grocery store requires diligent attention to brands, prices, labels, fat content, calories, while competing ads echo in our minds. Trivia. Even deciding what to wear is sometimes a problem, changing from aerobics, to work, to at-home, to evening clothes all in one day. Exhausting.

I compare my twentieth-century lifestyle and the importance of finding just the right brand of tennis shoes so my kids will be happy, with the mystics several centuries ago, and wonder whether such a simple existence is possible now, even among our rare cloistered monks and nuns. Perhaps it was always so, but our culture seems to demand focus on materiality, while our souls are starving. Just getting along from day to day, we seem to become covered with the pitch of the world, and like tar, materialism is difficult to get rid of. We walk around getting stuck to things that are not important to our salvation.

Whirligigs of Hope

At the cellular level, the experiential level, the cultural level, we struggle with the duality of our natures, trying to coordinate physical life with inner spirituality. As the cells of our bodies age and die; as we train ourselves to look for the shafts of Godlight piercing through the forests of our daily, ordinary lives; as we pray for peace in the grocery store—we call on a power greater than ourselves, greater than the pull of *chronos* on our dying physical natures, greater than the power of advertising: the Holy Spirit. Pain becomes joy, frustrations no longer chafe. Paul sums it up best in 2 Corinthians 4:16–18:

> Though our outer nature is wasting away, our inner nature is being renewed every day . . . because we look not to the things that are seen but to the things that are unseen; for the things that are seen are transient, but the things that are unseen are eternal.

We are dust and wind. We are earthly clay animated by the breath of God. On a spiritual journey, we become whirligigs of hope, dancing down the road toward everlasting life.

As we whirl along the road, we are also faced with two other contradictions pulling us in opposite directions: the need for solitude (and the temptation to crowd our lives with the urgent), and the need for community. Finding a balance between these two extremes is another demanding spiritual challenge.

Almighty and everlasting God, you made the universe with all its marvelous order, its atoms, worlds, and galaxies, and the infinite complexity of living creatures: Grant that, as we probe the mysteries of your creation, we may come to know you more truly, and more surely fulfill our role in your eternal purpose; in the name of Jesus Christ our Lord. Amen.

(THE BOOK OF COMMON PRAYER, *page 827*)

7

Between Busyness and Loneliness:
Finding a Garden of Solitude

In contemporary society our Adversary majors in three things:
noise, hurry, and crowds. If he can keep us engaged in
'muchness' and 'manyness,' he will rest satisfied. . . . (13)
—*Richard J. Foster,* CELEBRATION OF DISCIPLINE

When I was in graduate school, I had to read several postmodern
novels, many of which force the reader to suffer through hundreds
of pages of nonsense. But that's the point for postmodern writers:
Life itself makes no sense. Postmodern novels are crowded with
words, words, words, leading nowhere.

I hate postmodern novels.

They remind me too much of how my life gets when I do not
take the time to become centered spiritually.

Busyness vs. Loneliness

Consider the dilemma for many active people. Our commitments
start out as gentle hands extended with the promise of something
interesting. Often when we decide to have children, we have no

clue of the demands on our time and energy childrearing takes to do the job right. We sign up for that committee at church because the chairman promises it's only once a month, and it's for a good cause. Pretty soon, the gentle hands begin to grasp us, encircling our throats, and soon we are choking to death from all our duties and activities, wondering why we can't breathe spiritually, even though we may be at the church more than ever.

I juggle two part-time jobs in the mornings and run Mom's Taxi Service for two children in the afternoons—besides being a minister's wife and actively involved at Holy Trinity Church. Between family, work, and church, I lead a life-and-a-half, as do many of the people I know. More and more of my women friends have part-time or full-time jobs besides taking care of their families, and the women who do not work outside the home are often busier than those of us who do. This is not just a woman's problem, either, because many of our men friends take leading roles in the church, the community, and in the lives of their children as soccer coaches, Cub Scout leaders, and even cooks and bottle washers at home. I find, too, that many of my single friends also participate in this mania for action.

For me, these are the crowded years.

In contrast, I remember my grandmother, widowed, alone until she was almost ninety, rocking in the sunroom of her large, two-story home surrounded by a wrap-around porch and a silence so profound you could almost hear the photos crackling with age in their albums, the dust collecting behind the books in the sunroom's library. She never complained of loneliness. She didn't have to. Her house creaked and groaned it for her.

When I was in college, I used to visit my grandmother. As the thrumming vibes of Credence Clearwater Revival, Three Dog Night, and the Moody Blues echoed in my ears, I sat with Mamah as she rocked in the silence. I looked at her sparse white hair and her patterned dust coat and slippers, and thought with dismay, *How can she stand this lack of noise? How does she rock here day in and day out, reading occasionally, watching snippets of television* (she loved Elvis Presley). *What if I end up like her in an asylum of quietude?*

Now, of course, in the melee of my life, I envy her the quiet.

Solitude as an Antidote

Busyness and loneliness are not necessarily age-related, but rather are outward manifestations of an inward yearning/rankling occurring at any time in a life cycle. Though they appear to be opposite in nature, they really stem from the same spiritual problem: an untended garden at the center of our being. Like *The Secret Garden,* our souls are the innermost private places of our relationship with Christ. We have the key and can choose to let others in or not—or to let God in or not. When we get too busy, the garden becomes overgrown and choked with weeds; when we are lonely, the plants have died. In both cases, we need to spend more time in the garden, nourishing the flowers as we nourish the relationship with Christ.

Henri Nouwen discusses three movements of the spiritual life in his book *Reaching Out:* from hostility to hospitality, from illusion to prayer, and from loneliness to solitude. He suggests that we develop "solitude of heart," an "inner quality or attitude that does not depend on physical isolation" (25). For me, the poles of busyness on one hand and loneliness on the other represent the extremes between which we need to chart our course, to find "solitude of heart." God calls us to be active in others' lives; He also calls us to be alone. The balance between community and solitude is a delicate one, because both are necessary for our spiritual well-being. When we wander too far in either direction, our lives get out of kilter.

It seems both busyness and loneliness are often imposed on us externally. Sometimes we seem to have no control. For example, two co-chairs of one of the annual Methodist events admitted after it was over that they'd been snookered into the job. The person recruiting each had played one against the other: "She said she'd do it if you said you'd do it," including in her pitch other unspoken but irresistible temptations as well. "If you don't do this job, we'll have to cancel a ten-year tradition, and it will be your fault. This is a city-wide event and just think of the good publicity for the church. Hungry children won't get fed if you can't help raise the money."

Guiltily, the two women felt they couldn't turn down the job. It was "imposed" on them—or so it seemed.

Likewise, consider the recycling drives, the cookie sales, the sports events, the meetings after work, the *de rigeur* cocktail parties, and so on that fill up our calendars with scrawls of blue ink. "I *have* to go. My job depends on it." "We *need* to participate. Our child will feel excluded if we don't." Life's demands crash through the walls of our privacy, gobbling up our minutes, hours, days, weeks, years, eventually invading every cubic inch of our souls.

The dilemma of loneliness can also be rationalized by outward circumstances. "My husband left me, and nobody wants a single at dinner parties." "Old people just get in the way." "This is a family church, and a single man really doesn't belong." "I'm too shy to go to the Discovery Weekend without my spouse. What will I say to people?" We use things "beyond our control" as an excuse to stay at home, longing for human companionship, yet not willing to trade the familiar pangs of loneliness for the risk of encounters with people we don't know well.

God calls us to both community and solitude. Yet it is difficult not to get mauled by circumstances' shoving us too far in either direction. However, we *do* have some degree of control; though

God controls the seas, the weather, and the currents, we are the ones at the helm. Greek literature provides the perfect image of what happens as we sail through life. On his return voyage to Ithaca, Odysseus has to steer his ship between the six-headed monster, Scylla, on one bank of the isthmus and the whirlpool of Charybdis near the other. Scylla, the monster, is like the loneliness that can devour us if we get too close, and Charybdis is the whirlpool of activities that sucks us under if we aren't careful. Like Odysseus, we must steer our lives between the two if we are to reach our destinations safely. Fortunately, we are at the mercy of a kind God who wants to help us to steer clear of both disasters, if we ask Him.

Jacob's Balance

What about Jacob? What is his struggle in the question of community versus solitude? Jacob arrived at the border of Edom. He remembered that God had told him that his descendants would be "as the sand of the sea, which cannot be numbered for multitude" (Genesis 32:12), and he was well on his way, surrounded by his household. The context of his life was his extended family, and from this family, a great nation would emerge. His life was to be lived among them.

The day before Jacob wrestled with God, he waved good-bye to his family, standing by himself on the other side of the stream. "And Jacob was left alone" (Genesis 32:24). *Alone* is the key word here. Only when he was *alone* did God come to him.

Jacob had achieved the right balance for a spiritual encounter with the living God. He lived in a context of community, participating fully in his family and in his society's obligations and demands; he did not wander alone through life, uninvolved in the lives of other people. Yet in a time of crisis, he separated himself from his family, from even his closest members. In order to encounter God, he needed to be alone.

The goal is spiritual balance, an impossible feat to manage unless we continually tend the inner garden with prayer, tossing distractions back over the wall as they invade our privacy. If we scurry about, doing God's work in the world without time for reflection, then we get out of sorts with ourselves, our children, and the people to whom we're trying to minister. When my life is crowded, I resent grading papers, I do not have time to play Candyland, and dinner comes out of a box. That I am doing the "work of the Lord" is slim consolation when I don't even have time to say hello to my Maker, or to watch and listen to what He is trying to show me through each item on a hastily crossed-off list.

The great temptation is to think that an unbalanced life is not a serious problem, and not a life-threatening disease. Big mistake.

The Necessity of Reflection

A friend commented once that she went through her days taking imaginary pictures, snapshots of the important moments, and it was essential to her health and well-being that she take the time at some point to sort through the photos. If she couldn't carve out time during the day, then her mind insisted on it at night. Instead of falling asleep from exhaustion, though her body craved rest, her mind forced her to sift through the day, evaluating, understanding, coming to terms with the events and encounters.

For those seeking to deepen our lives in Christ, to bring all of our lives before Him, reflection is necessary. To carry the analogy further, we must sit with Him in a garden of solitude, showing Him the snapshots of our daily lives and discussing them with Him, asking what they mean, what He wants to show us. The process for me goes something like this. One crazy Saturday, we woke the kids early to get them to an Eddie Coker concert downtown. At the concert, I saw a friend who had a tumor the size of a grapefruit growing in her lung and whose heart had been displaced near her navel on the right side of her body. She had just returned from a near-fatal bout of pneumonia in the hospital. I hugged her and asked how she was doing. "Blessed!" she answered. "I woke up this morning with energy. I knew how much my son wanted to come to this concert, and I'm so grateful God gave me the energy to get out of bed. I am truly blessed."

In the middle of a hundred young children gyrating and singing "I Am the Happy One," I watched my friend sitting near me, eyes closed with a smile on her face. Her body was dying, but her spirit was growing closer and closer to God. How could I not be moved deeply by the testimony of her life? How could I not take the time to push away the happy noise of the children and pray for her healing and for my own gratitude for her life and witness? Fortunately, we carry the garden around with us, and we can enter the walls of silence and solitude even when surrounded by others.

As we lurched to the next event, the Cub Scout food collection, I realized we had a small task force to cover a large neighborhood. Following my children in the car as they gathered the sacks of food from porches and driveways and put them in the pick-up truck ahead of me, I felt pressure: We would have to abandon the Cub Scouts if we were to meet my husband on time.

Finally, (why is it that I so rarely think of this first?) I opened the garden gate and said to God, "You're going to have to handle the time problem here because I've bungled all the arrangements." He did, of course. In addition, once I had released my own agenda and opened that gate, I looked around me with unworried, unclouded eyes. My children scampered happily down the street, and

I remembered with a pang all those childless years. Gratefulness trickled down like a spring shower, and as we turned corner after corner, I thanked God for these precious children darting from house to house. Also, I became aware that this neighborhood—not a wealthy neighborhood by any stretch of the imagination—was turning out sack after sack of food. I was amazed and grateful for the generosity of people, the average citizens who never get on TV because they live quiet and decent lives.

We left the Cub Scouts on the last street; then we picked up my husband and dashed back downtown to the Festival of Trees at the convention center, where thousands of people jostled through vendor's booths, displays, shows, jugglers, and games for the children. A madhouse. Just the sort of affair my children love. Just the sort of affair I can't stand after the first fifteen minutes. Even in that mayhem, my camera caught a moment I later understood more fully. The head of the event (a woman who goes to our church) sat in a folding chair away from the crowd on the floor of the convention center, cradling her three-year-old child, patting her gently, and talking to her as if she had nothing else to do all day.

This was a woman doing it right. She had walled herself and her hurting child in an invisible place of comfort among throngs of people whose pleasure she was responsible for.

Finally, after I had taken my daughter to her birthday party, I rushed from store to store. I felt my muscles begin to tighten as the elusive Christmas gifts remained out of my reach. I began to resent having to buy these Christmas gifts, letting the resentment leak over onto the entire season of Christmas. What a Scrooge! Instead, how much nicer the time would have been if I'd prayed at the stoplights instead of scowling, and if I'd spent time being grateful for the gifts' recipients. However, this insight didn't come to me until later reflection, when I realized that nobody but me really cared what I got my loved ones for Christmas. They would be happy with anything. Once again, I could have spent time in the garden instead of hacking through the tangled vines of my own desire to provide the "perfect" gift.

How We Miss God's Gifts

The point is this. Often, if we barrel through our days with no reflection and without listening to God's voice in the middle of the bustling, niggling, babbling pother, then we miss both His presence (an enormous gift in itself), and we miss His other gifts bestowed on us simply because we are alive on the earth. Ralph Waldo Emerson wrote in his journal in 1847, on the eve of his birthday: "The days come and go like muffled and veiled figures sent from a distant friendly party, but they say nothing, and if we do not use the gifts they bring, they carry them as silently away" (419). We are considerably poorer if we do not take the time to be with God in the garden, asking Him to interpret the gifts budding, ready to bloom in every event of our lives.

Henri Nouwen, in *Making All Things New: An Invitation to the Spiritual Life,* suggests that the problem is not the sheer amount of activities we participate in, but our inner attitude.

> Jesus does not respond to our worry-filled way of living by saying that we should not be so busy with worldly affairs. He does not try to pull us away from the many events, activities, and people that make up our lives . . . .
>
> He asks us to shift the point of gravity, to relocate the center of our attention, to change our priorities. . . . Jesus does not speak about a change of activities, a change in contacts, or even a change of pace. He speaks about a change of heart. This change of heart makes everything different, even while everything appears to be the same. (25)

This change of heart occurs when we take the time for solitude.

Dying people often have a keener sense of the necessity of time spent alone in prayer. Once-crucial commitments fade like mist. One woman was about to undergo a serious operation after fighting cancer for many years. She explained to her friends, eager to help, support, and love her, that she was posting a "No Visitors" sign on her door, not because she was trying to be unfriendly, but because she needed to be alone with God in the hospital room. She wanted to turn the room into a garden.

The ultimate garden is, of course, Gethsemane. I have always thought it ironic that Jesus spent His blood-sweating agony not on an ash heap like Job, or in the desert like the Israelites, but instead among blossoms and the fresh scent of cedar and olive trees. After the Last Supper, He did not choose to impart more wisdom to His disciples; he did not choose to be in intimate contact with those He loved the most. He chose to be alone with God, and this fragrant garden was the spot He picked to wrestle out His destiny before His Father.

I've also thought it was ironic that, although He entered the garden alone, He asked His friends to wait for Him, to keep watch. They didn't, of course; they abandoned Him by falling asleep. We learn two important things from this story. First, we are wise to follow Jesus' model and go before God alone, especially with those issues that tear us apart. Second, we are all abandoned at times, our loneliness accentuated by friends who cannot stay awake with us in our struggles.

Back to postmodern literature. Though I don't trust or believe their primary message, these authors do have one point: If we stumble through our busy lives without reflection and prayer, things really do become like a jumbled bunch of words with no meaning. We begin to babble, and things do not make sense.

Turning Loneliness from a Curse to a Blessing

What about the other side of the coin—loneliness? What about people who have all the time in the world to live in a garden, but who still feel empty and alone? Fighting for time alone is a very different thing from having aloneness forced on us. The very thing we may be wrestling with in the garden could be feelings of loneliness.

Although I have mixed feelings now, like many Americans, I have traditionally been a fan of Diana, Princess of Wales. When we visited St. Paul's in London, I passed by all that historical stuff and headed straight for the wedding display. Before her divorce became final, she gave a controversial interview on A&E TV. She made a memorable comment concerning the deep loneliness she'd experienced as a member of England's royal family: "There's no better way to dismantle a personality than to isolate it." She spoke with wisdom from the experience of having felt dismantled and isolated within her own home.

You don't have to be Princess of Wales to experience loneliness. We commoners have been in this place of isolation too. Every time my husband and I have moved—especially when we moved from Texas to Washington, D.C.—I have suffered feelings of emptiness, aching for friends and family. Sunday afternoons when Stockton studied at the seminary library, I took the Metro into Washington, D.C. and haunted the museums by myself.

This ache of aloneness is so intense that we place all kinds of buffers, like bulwarks, to stave it away. In fact, the person with too much to do may be fighting against the terror of being lonely, as though a crowd of things to do will hide, or disguise, the emptiness at the center.

American literature during the first half of this century was filled with characters suffering from loneliness and alienation from others and from their own feelings. Hemingway's characters wandered aimlessly all over Europe, drinking in bars and having empty encounters with each other in railway stations. In F. Scott Fitzgerald's *The Great Gatsby*, we can all picture Jay Gatsby's loneliness in his stone mansion, throwing huge, wild parties, hoping to lure Daisy back into his life.

Is there a cure? Is there a way to shoo away the negative feelings associated with abandonment, exclusion, shyness, rejection? A friend of ours shared a pre-Christmas experience which helped him feel a little less alone:

> The morning of December 12, 1995, was typical of a frantic holiday household with a list of errands without adequate time. While loading the car, I set the file containing 150+ pages of Liturgy and Worship Council minutes and notes on the roof of the car.
>
> I had driven less than two blocks when the rearview mirror reflected the pages scattered the length and breadth of Golf Course Road. Not only did I have to stop and pick them up, but everyone passing would know what this fool had done.
>
> I had dodged traffic for the longest ninety seconds of my life, when three cars pulled over and three total strangers began to help me. Both east and westbound traffic came to a halt as these three good Samaritans restored the pages, and my faith in my fellow man. Their actions reset the tone of what became a truly wonderful season, and reminded me that I wasn't alone, and never had been.

Our friend received a gift, a reminder that we live in community, and that God sends us people in our lives at moments when we need them. Yet sometimes we need to seek the reminder for ourselves. Fortunately, we have always at our fingertips the Bible, and the Scriptures are honest about the very real problem of loneliness. As my husband once said in a talk on aloneness, the Scriptures show "aloneness laid bare."

Loneliness in the Bible

In several individual laments, the psalmist seems to be alone, surrounded by enemies. He calls upon God to show His face, to relieve the misery. For example, in Psalm 102, the psalmist begs, "Hear my prayer, O Lord; let my cry come to thee! Do not hide thy face from me in the day of my distress! . . . I lie awake, I am like a lonely bird on the housetop. All the day my enemies taunt me." The psalmist is not the first nor the last human being to lie awake at night, alone, trying to fend off feelings of despair, abandonment, rejection.

Next to the Gospels, my favorite part of the Bible is the psalms because the psalmist is so human. When he's in pain, he's groaning; when he's rejoicing, the earth cannot contain his joy. The psalmist doesn't try to gloss over loneliness. He knows it hurts. Yet time after time, after he's wailed to God in his pain, he is able to come around to a position of hope. Psalm 22, part of which Jesus quoted on the cross, most dramatically describes the lowest depth of loneliness: "My God, my God, why hast thou forsaken me?" Not only does the psalmist (and Jesus) have no friends or family to help dispel the angst of despair, but even God seems to have abandoned Him. Yet even this psalm of deep loneliness ends with a note of faith in the Lord: "Men shall tell of the Lord to the coming generation, and proclaim his deliverance to a people yet unborn, that he has wrought it."

These and psalms like them provide a pattern for our spiritual lives. Yes, it's okay to moan when we hurt. We must tell God how we feel; it's part of the process of healing. When we feel we've been abandoned, or hurt, or rejected by our friends and family, we need to weep. Then we need to continue the conversation. We need to stay in the garden, talking with God. After we have bewailed our situation, we need to remember that God's Spirit fills the deepest wells of hurt. We need to keep talking until our pain loses its edge, until we can see the tiny shoots of hope pricking through the soil. When I run out of my own words, I read the words of the psalms—out loud if I need to. The point is to keep talking.

Another biblical example of loneliness is Job. When we are looking for examples of how to survive suffering, Job provides the gold standard. One of the many things he endured on the ash heap scraping his scabs with a potsherd was loneliness. Early on, his wife abandoned his struggle, telling him to curse God and die. His three friends were no help at all, scrambling the issue and blaming him unjustly for his troubles. Nobody understood Job, providing him with a poignant loneliness on top of his other troubles.

> He [God] has put my brethren far from me,
> and my acquaintances are wholly estranged from me.
> My kinsfolk and my close friends have failed me;
> the guests in my house have forgotten me;
> my maidservants count me as a stranger . . .
> I am repulsive to my wife,
> loathsome to the sons of my own mother.
> Even young children despise me. . . . (JOB 19:13–17)

In this passage, Job claims that *God has caused his isolation.* What are we to make of this? From what we know of God, He does not heap bad things on us or even allow them to happen in His permissive will, unless He plans to heap good things on us as a result. Even dying has a reward so great we can't fathom it. In Job's case, he is granted not the wisdom or the understanding of why the bad things happened to him, why he sat on the ash heap so lonely, but Job is granted the most precious gift of all: He is one of the few people in the Bible who saw God face to face and lived.

In the thunder of God's words as He addresses Job, the questions disappear. The loneliness disappears. The despair disappears. In earthly terms, he is granted blessings too. His fortunes and prosperity and health (and presumably his relationships with friends and family) return. If God had not allowed Job to experience intense loneliness, He would not have been ready for the greatest gift of all—the presence of God breaking into his life.

For us, loneliness can be the prelude for great spiritual fullness.

Consider the apostle Paul. Like Jesus at his trial, his friends deserted him. He writes in 2 Timothy 4:10–11 of all who have abandoned him; only Luke is with him. He says: "At my first defense no one took my part; all deserted me. May it not be charged against them! But the Lord stood by me and gave me strength to proclaim the word fully. . . ."

Again the pattern is clear. Though we may stand alone, deserted by friends and family, God does not leave us. We need to stay in communication with God, and He will fill the holes of our emptiness with His presence. As He did for Paul, and for Job eventually, God will also place people in our lives to ease the ache of loneliness.

Praying in the Garden

We know we need to make space for a dialogue, but the questions arise: What do we say to God in the garden? How do we learn to listen?

I have a friend who says beautiful prayers. The way she lifts her praises and words her requests used to give me an inferiority complex when it was my turn to pray aloud after her. I am a very blunt person, whose needs and expressions of love are starkly practical and immediate. I cannot elaborate in beautiful language like my friend. My song of praise is like giving God a present in a paper sack instead of a beautifully wrapped package. Still, I am sincere and diligent.

I picture my friend's time with Jesus in the garden as a leisurely stroll among lush blossoms hanging down from the walls, sprouting lavishly from every growing bush, with exotic plants thriving in every crevice.

I have another friend who is into meditation, who goes regularly on long weekends of silence. I picture this garden as well-trimmed, beautifully landscaped, with birds singing.

For myself, I've got simple tools, like an old spade; and my garden contains a hodgepodge of plants. It's not lush, nor is it landscaped, and I constantly fight weeds. But at least it's growing—a feat for which I am daily grateful. I used to feel envy for those whose prayers were "better" than mine, for people who had a strict regular hour of meditation, or for those who said the daily office every day. But then I realized *that there is no such thing as an inferior prayer.* Awkward prayers, tongue-tied prayers, prayers from a dry well, prayers from a giddy heart, even show-off prayers all have validity, not because of the *prayee,* but because of the Recipient. The thing is to keep talking, and when you run out of words, sit tight on a rock and listen. Just don't walk away.

Many books have been written about different styles of prayers for different personality types. Thank goodness! Just as every person is unique in our freckled, hairy, smooth-cheeked way, so is every prayer garden different. Our responsibility is not what to say or how to say it—the Holy Spirit prays when we do not have the words—but to clear the space in our lives for the conversation to take place.

Living and Dying, Alone before God

Whether we come from lives currently crowded with people and activities or lives silent and resounding with loneliness, we need to accept one thing, trite as it sounds. We are born alone, and we die alone. The crises of our lives are experienced alone in private moments of truth. And it is when we are alone that God can truly touch and transform our souls.

Therefore, our aloneness is one of the greatest gifts we have. God created us as unique beings, and what's even more exciting than being an individual work of art is that God wants to spend time with us. He allows us to be lonely so we will seek Him, and He probably misses us when we avoid Him by packing the suitcases of our lives with stuff we can't take with us.

In fact, another one of the benefits of spending time in the garden with God is that when we inevitably die, we have the feeling we are going home instead of to some stranger's house because we have already spent so much time in the place where He lives. Through the gift of aloneness, God cuddles us, challenges us, entertains us, instructs us, and lets us get to know Him. Time alone with God—peaceful, quiet time as well as the time of deep wrestling—is like dating before marriage. Looking at death as the consummation of our earthly lives, if we have not spent time with our beloved beforehand, then we are like mail-order brides thrust suddenly into a strange household. It seems that we come to know our Savior most deeply, most intimately when we have struggled with Him alone, like Jacob in the desert.

The passage in Matthew 25:29, where Jesus says, "For to every one who has will more be given, and he will have abundance; but from him who has not, even what he has will be taken away" has always bothered me—until I figured out He was referring to spiritual things. If we are willing to spend much time talking with

God in the garden, then the gifts He gives us bloom into the next yard; if we give Him only a tiny bit of our time and energy, then our gardens die, and the flowers we do have wither.

The classic literary illustration of what we can and cannot take with us when we die comes from the medieval drama, *Everyman*. Everyman, like many of us, has spent his life going about his business and staying out of trouble. When it's time for his journey to the grave, he finds that item by item, his loved ones, his friends, his money, his looks, his physical strength, his mind—in fact, all the things he held dearer than God in his life—fall away. Only his good deeds stay with him. Every barrier between himself and his Maker must be knocked out from under him before he can meet God.

Whether we like the fact or not, death is a journey we take by ourselves. In spite of C. S. Lewis' delightful book, *The Great Divorce*, which takes a busload of tourists to the next life, we do not ascend to heaven via mass transportation. If we have spent time cultivating our relationship with Jesus, then the idea of aloneness—to say nothing of the idea of death—is not nearly so frightening.

When my father-in-law lay dying in the hospital, the social worker told us that many people, especially those surrounded by loved ones on a death watch, will wait until everyone leaves the room before they die. Even patients in a coma will sense the absence of the family member, who has rushed to the cafeteria for five minutes to grab a sandwich. Many, many times, the disappointed relative comes back to find the patient gone.

I find it fascinating that human beings so often sense the need to be alone with God, and will wait for that moment of aloneness before allowing themselves to make the transition from earth into the next life. Since one day we will all teeter on the threshold of that moment of transition, I find it comforting to spend time *now* with the One into whose hands we will, like Jesus, ultimately commend our spirits.

Avoiding Intimacy with God

So why do I fight it? What perversity in my nature allows me to cook the bacon, make the bed, and get half my make-up on before I stop and say, "Good morning! Thank You for another day!" to my Maker. Why do I stew over worldly things, spending several hours in a tailspin over what menu to serve the Vestry? Even when I have a major theological issue I know I need to thrash out before God, why do I wait until two in the morning before dragging my pillows to the couch to do the serious wrestling?

I don't know. Except I do know that those intense moments alone with God are not always fun. Sometimes the garden is lovely and peaceful and fragrant. But sometimes, the wind blows so hard the limbs fall off the trees and the flowers rip right off the bushes. Sometimes He wants us to replant our favorite foliage, and sometimes He just lets us sit there, listening to the wind howl.

We are vulnerable when we stand before God. We are naked. We have been carefully trained not to allow ourselves to be exposed in our weakness, and our great temptation is to place buffers between ourselves and the God who can see us with no clothes on. Our families, other people, jobs, even our church work keep us busy with the illusion that if we streak through life, maybe God won't have time to examine us closely.

Because the experience of the soul's aloneness before God can be uncomfortable, even painful, we certainly wouldn't wish it on anybody else. So we force ourselves in well-meaning ways between other people and God. Like Job's friends, we talk too much and say the wrong things when our friends are in grief. We flood hospital rooms. We are afraid to let silences fall in our conversations. We rush to save people from the loneliness we fear on their behalf.

We hide from God, and help others to hide, in the bushes of the Garden of Eden, covering ourselves with skimpy fig leaves and other shreds of inadequate foliage from the growth of our busy lives.

And yet. . . . We cannot forget that we are called to live our lives as Christians in community with other Christians. Sometimes we are called to break into another person's loneliness, bringing God's presence with us. We are called to come together and worship with each other, allowing the Holy Spirit to move through us as a group. Powerful moments also occur in the context of worship, and in prayer and praise with other Christians.

However, the principle remains the same: It is possible to sit in church reviewing our list of things to do instead of creating the solitude of heart necessary for worship. Though our bodies may be kneeling in community, we still have not cleared the garden space inside. No matter where we are, who we are with, creating the heart of solitude is still a matter of getting alone with God.

Turning Aloneness into a Gift

I would like to close this chapter with a story from *Dream a New Dream: How to Rebuild a Broken Life* by Dale Galloway, a story of a shy, quiet little boy who turned the kind of aloneness we all fear into joy. Every day, Chad's mother agonized when she saw the big group of kids walking home from school, with Chad trailing along after them.

Near Valentine's Day, Chad announced to his mother that he wanted to make a valentine for everybody in his class. His mother's heart sank, but Chad was insistent, so she went out and bought the colors and paper and glue. For several weeks, Chad and his mother made thirty-five valentines.

On Valentine's Day, Chad skipped happily off to school with the valentines. That afternoon, Chad's mother put out cookies and milk and watched out the window as the children came home, Chad lingering alone behind them as usual. The other children were laughing and talking, but Chad's arms were empty. Obviously, he had received no valentines, and she expected him to cry when he walked inside the door. In fact, she hid her own tears when he came in. But Chad walked right by the cookies and milk, his face glowing. "Not a one. Not a one," he said.

His mother's heart ached. Then he added, "I didn't forget a one, Mommy. Not a single one" (77–8).

How many of us can say we've allowed God to turn our aloneness into such a rich, full experience?

O God, in the course of this busy life, give us times of refreshment and peace; and grant that we may so use our leisure to rebuild our bodies and renew our minds, that our spirits may be opened to the goodness of your creation; through Jesus Christ our Lord. Amen.

(THE BOOK OF COMMON PRAYER, *page 825*)

Almighty God, whose Son had nowhere to lay his head: Grant that those who live alone may not be lonely in their solitude, but that, following in his steps, they may find fulfillment in loving you and their neighbors; through Jesus Christ our Lord. Amen.

(THE BOOK OF COMMON PRAYER, *page 829*)

8

Death
and Forgiveness

I do not die. . .
I leave the land of the dying.
—EDWARD THE CONFESSOR, ON HIS DEATHBED

On March 29, 1992 in Kerrville, Texas, an elderly couple, Juliana and Clayton, had finished a Sunday meal of chili and homemade cornbread made by Juliana's daughter, Adrienne. Adrienne had just helped her mother, a stroke victim, into her chair in front of the television when the doorbell rang. Clayton shuffled to the door and opened it.

Two teenage boys, high on speed, rushed in and one of them cracked Clayton's skull with a tire iron. When Adrienne ran over to help defend her stepfather, the other boy beat her over the head with a cedar post. While Juliana screamed, helpless, from her chair across the room, the two boys repeatedly crushed Clayton's and Adrienne's skulls with multiple blows.

Then they attacked Juliana.

It took thirty minutes for Juliana, Adrienne, and Clayton to die. Finally, just to make sure, the boys returned from the kitchen with a knife and stabbed them each nine or ten times in the throat. They stole a spoon collection and a few knick-knacks. The bodies lay in the dark all night before the housekeeper discovered them the next morning.

My sister woke up to the news on the radio. The media had reached her before we'd been called by the authorities. Next of kin had been Juliana's sister—my other aunt, Millie—and Millie hadn't had the chance to call the rest of the family before the story came out over the air.

Adrienne had been my closest cousin. She was nearest my age, and we had been roommates several years before.

My sister saw the pictures taken by the police. As she said in despair after viewing photos so bloody she couldn't make out arms or legs, much less faces: *We have no category for this.*

A major question became how to live in a world where people stroll into your house and kill you and drive away.

An even more difficult question was raised the first night after the family and friends gathered in Kerrville. Sitting in the gracious dining room of the Hilton, we listened to soft elevator music, and tried unsuccessfully to make civilized conversation without referring to the blood spattered all over the walls and floor of my family's home. Knowing my husband was a priest, one of my cousin's friends turned to me over coffee, and with red-rimmed, bloodshot eyes, said, "I suppose you're going to try to forgive whoever killed them."

Caught off-guard by her intensity, I stumbled around and said, "Well, yes. I suppose I have to. Sooner or later."

She leveled those eyes at me and whispered, "As long as I live, I will *never, ever* forgive the person who did this."

As it turned out, my reaction has been closer to hers than to my initial pious response. It took weeks and months for the full horror of the crime to settle in, and as the implications sank deeper and deeper, so did my rage.

The issue of forgiveness surrounding death became a live and many-tentacled thing, like an octopus. Just when I thought I had resolved one issue of forgiveness, a different issue wrapped itself around my neck. Death itself is traumatic enough to come to terms with, but forgiveness—forgiveness has come hard, incompletely, and in many difficult stages.

Though the death of my three relatives was more shocking and traumatic than most deaths, the issues of dying and forgiveness arise even, say, when an elderly relative passes away peacefully after a long, fruitful life. Death is still the final word on earth, and forgiveness still requires faith and the serious trowel work of self-examination.

Obstacles to Forgiveness

My aunt Juliana had been a black-haired beauty with a white streak in front and a widow's peak. Adrienne was her only child. In her mid-forties and successful in several careers, Adrienne had moved back to Kerrville to help her mother because Clayton at eighty-three had become too frail to lift Juliana in and out of her chair.

That night in March as she sat trapped in her chair, waiting for the killers to reach her, Juliana may have been spared complete horror. The autopsy report indicated that she had suffered a second stroke, and our prayer is that by a sliver of mercy, she died before having to witness the full extent of such bloody business.

How do you forgive someone for doing that to an old lady?

The two intruders had scoped out the house, targeting Juliana and Clayton because they lived in a lovely home, featured in national decorator magazines, and because they were old and weak. The first obstacle to forgiveness was the sheer bestiality of the crime, placing it in a separate classification altogether, a slot different from most forgivable deeds. The break-in should have been a simple burglary. However, this is the end of the twentieth century and violence is on the rise.

We soon found we were not alone in having relatives murdered. Far too many people suffer from this kind of inhuman brutality these days, and getting on with life for survivors is a delicate art, an act of grace. The initial reaction to animal behavior is animal outrage. Only later can God's grace filter back into the dark place carved from such pain. Inevitably, the first reaction to violence is, "This crime is too terrible to forgive."

The next obstacle in the process of forgiveness was the fact that the killers remained at large for over a year. Just as there was no focus for the anger, so there was no focus for forgiveness. Knowing a perpetrator skulked "out there" somewhere, unidentified, used to make me crazy. That he'd gotten away with the crime only fueled my desperation. I needed a scapegoat, a person, to pin my hate and anger on.

Further, with no evidence, the police began to "blame" my relatives, reconstructing a fight scene with a former disgruntled employee, wrongly suspected from the first. A Texas Ranger called the murders a "grudge deal," and reporters all over the state hinted darkly at a nasty argument.

No! No matter what words had been exchanged (and, of course, they had not), my relatives did not deserve to be murdered. Nor did the victims deserve to be blamed for causing their own deaths. Blaming them was like saying a woman deserved to be raped because of the way she walked.

As the list of people to be forgiven grew, unforgiveness became a sack of misery lodged deep somewhere in my abdominal cavity. First the murderer. Then the police for suggesting that my relatives had brought their fate on themselves. Then the detectives for not finding the killers. Finally, the newspapers for reporting untruths, for slandering the innocent.

Anger

Not surprisingly, anger at God was a phase I went through. If God is all-powerful, why had He allowed this evil to take place? Not a single one of the theologians I'd pored over in seminary had answered to my satisfaction the question of God's permissive will. Now the issue had become personal. "Where were the angels? Why did God look the other way that night?" I cried to my husband. Juliana had been a committed Christian, and I could not see how He could allow such an awful thing to happen.

Then I remembered the cross, and how God had allowed His only Son to be murdered by a crowd of hooligans after blood. Where were the angels then? Held back, of course, because God had a plan more magnificent than either of the huddled figures of Mary or John could make out from the view at the bottom of the cross. I figured that night in Kerrville, God was probably as hurt and sad as we were, and I pictured Jesus weeping over these three as He did over His friend Lazarus.

Still, with nowhere to pin the anger, there was little hope of forgiveness either. I felt like the psalmist who wanted to dash someone against the rocks (Psalm 137). But who?

Justice vs. Revenge

I was teaching Hamlet to my sophomore English class at the University of Houston, and we were studying Hamlet's wavering attempts to avenge his father's murder. "What is the difference between revenge and justice?" I asked my students. It was not a rhetorical question. It was a very real issue for me. In my prayers, I asked God please to let the police catch the killers. I badly wanted them to pay for what they had done. But the darkness in my heart suggested that I was not after mere justice, but revenge. I wanted the killers to pay big-time. I wanted them to feel as miserable as they had made me feel. Revenge belongs to the Lord, but I wanted Him to take His full measure. Even though I knew that revenge could take many forms, including living in an inner hell, I couldn't swallow the galling possibility that the murderers might get away with their actions, scot-free from the justice system.

At any rate, the two young men were finally apprehended, thanks to Crime Stoppers. Now at last we had a focus for our anger, but the hope of forgiveness grew dimmer the more I knew about the circumstances and the criminals involved. They were *not* sorry, and admitted it on videotape. One had written a poem about watching my family die. One said that he'd enjoyed the "rush" he got, and that he'd done it "for the thrill of it." I shuddered: Calling these two men animals was too great a compliment. Animals kill for food, for protection, but not for a thrill.

More than ever, I wanted revenge, and I was terrified that the legal system would let these criminals go on a technicality.

I struggled a long time on my couch with this one. The first breakthrough I had in my spiritual life concerning these two young men occurred during the trial of the first one. We found out that he had been given marijuana when he was five years old, and was a full-fledged drug addict by the time he was ten. For the first time, I felt sorry for that little defenseless five-year-old. How could he have had a chance in life, given his poverty-stricken, drug-ridden upbringing?

And yet. He had made a series of choices as he grew older, increasing in violence and hatred. In the end, he was convicted and sentenced to death.

I was sick through most of the first trial. When the jury finally revealed its verdict, I felt a ponderous, unsatisfying relief. In my prayertime, as I thanked God that justice had been done (but still wondering why I didn't feel much better), a thought sliced through me: *In order to heal from this massacre, I need to pray for these two men.*

No, I said to God. *I cannot pray for these two people. Please don't ask me to do that. Please.*

Further Struggles

I continued to struggle. The trial of the second killer ended with a life sentence, and we had the privilege of watching our court system exonerate the second young man from personal responsibility for his actions. This boy was the brains behind the operation, who had targeted my family's house for robbery and planned the break-in for weeks.

Charging $360 an hour, a psychiatrist on sale to the highest bidder spent two days of the government's money explaining that the killer was simply "depressed," and "couldn't help" his premeditated act. The psychiatrist said that, in his opinion, if he'd had medication, this young man wouldn't have done it. The psychiatrist and the defense attorney took away the killer's responsibility for the action, his choice in the matter, and his hope of salvation. If he weren't responsible, and if he weren't sorry, how could he be forgiven? Repentance is required to enter heaven, and he was robbed of repentance. Fortunately, his forgiveness by God was none of my business.

His forgiveness by me, however, was.

In the meantime, two more people—the psychiatrist and the defense attorney—had joined the list of people I now needed to forgive. The worst part was that we knew both the psychiatrist and the defense attorney, and their actions seemed all the more personal than if they had been anonymous people just doing a job. By now a crowd pressed in, squelching all hope that I could grant any of them clemency or compassion.

For months, I fought the Holy Spirit over praying for these people, especially the killers. What they had done seemed unforgivable, no matter how pathetic their personal circumstances. I felt torn that the Holy Spirit had put this request in my heart. In the end, I made a deal, in tears. *All right, God,* I said in my most grudging, reluctant voice, the words pulled from me like skin being torn off my body. *All right, I'll pray for these two men. If You show Yourself to them, that they may see You and know You, maybe these three deaths would not be in vain.*

It is the best I can do for now. Healing for these deaths may take me the rest of my life—I still dream about my cousin, with her dark, curly hair and huge smile. At least now, I know the shape my prayers need to take. I picture my aunt's new glimmering, pain-free body, and am grateful she no longer suffers. Maybe she understands better than I do. Maybe, like Christ, she has forgiven these men. Maybe she is able to say, "This is the point. We killed Christ, and God forgives us for it." Maybe one day she will remind me, "By forgiving them, you forgive yourself."

Facing Death

The Kerrville slayings highlighted the problem of death and the related problem of forgiveness. From one day to the next, all the colors changed in my world and the tint of death dulled every aspect of my life: conversations with clerks at the grocery store, dialogue with students, playtime with the kids, neighborhood chats, theological discussions, TV selections, movies. Kerrville was the great divide in my life, after which nothing was the same.

Mid-life often brings a sharper awareness of death, but there's nothing like the shrill ring of the phone in the middle of the night to plunge us deep into its recesses. At some point, each of us must look death in the face, reconciling life as we know it with the promise of life as we don't yet understand it. We must tip our hat to the moment of death, the body's farewell spasm, the often painful hinge between two states of being. Because eleven of my family members died during a brief span of time, this issue has been pressed on me. I wouldn't have elected to deal with death this intimately by my own choice.

How many of us, though, get to pick the timing?

Jacob's fears and issues during the night of wrestling with God must surely have included the specter of death stomping around on the far bank of the stream. Esau had not gathered the four hundred armed men to be a welcoming party; as he'd rounded up the men and weapons, he was serious about killing his brother. I wonder if Jacob, alone in the dark, saw their many campfires flickering in the distance, or heard the men sharpening their knives and swords. Among the many fears Jacob faced that night, the very real possibility of dying must have been among them. He probably had other questions to thrash out as well: his own responsibility for the potential deaths of his family and household, for example, or whether he'd be willing to kill his brother if the battle narrowed to one-on-one combat, or whether his brother would choose to forgive him rather than carve him up.

Part of Jacob's struggle was his own unfinished business. Jews do not believe in heaven, but rather believe that they will live on in their offspring and in their deeds remembered. Jacob had a keen sense that God's promise to him hadn't been completed. In prayer, he reminded God of this: *Didn't You promise to return me to my kindred and to do me good?* (Genesis 32:9). Jacob didn't have the hope of resurrection as we do, but he had God's promise for fulfillment.

If Jacob could have read his own obituary, he would have been much comforted. He might also have gleaned some insights on how his life impacted others.

Nicholas Halasz, in Robert Raines' book *Creative Brooding*, tells the story of Alfred Nobel, who woke up one morning and read his own obituary. A French reporter had printed it by mistake, confusing Alfred with his brother, who had died. Alfred had spent his life inventing dynamite, then making a fortune off of weapons of destruction. In the obituary, he was described as the "Dynamite King"; the world would remember him as a "merchant of death." When he read the story of his life, Alfred was horrified and decided to make the world aware that he was a different kind of person. "The result was the most valued of prizes, given to those who have done most for the cause of world peace" and other worthy achievements (121).

One of the most important things we can do in facing our own death is to look hard at what people might say about us when we die. Do our actions reflect our spiritual lives?

Death as Both Obstacle and Gateway

In my moments of deepest clarity—those few times in prayer when I can glimpse pebbles of truth nestled under the water at the bottom of the swimming hole—I know death to be the gateway to Paradise. I'm comfortable with the notion that we all will die. I accept happily the abstraction that we'll be better off in the next world. Yet for most of us, getting to Paradise is not like stepping up into a place of exquisite beauty; the transition experience is more like invading the beaches of Normandy.

Though death has been conquered by Christ on the cross, we still sweat it out.

The moment of death (the "M. O. D.," my sister calls it) is not what I fear, but I dread the circumstances, the suffering, the choice of timing, the possibility of horrible surprise, the unpreparedness, the not-knowing when that moment will take place. I've watched too many people die not to know we're better off in heaven; I've watched too many people die not to know also that climbing up the mountain toward heaven can be slow and agonizing until we cross the border.

Non-Christians often see the moment of death as the moment of extinction. For us, it is the moment Real Life begins. Like cicadas, we shed the husks of bothersome bodies, and scamper into infinity in our risen bodies, bare-armed and forgiven, facing a merciful judgment from a God who loves us more than we can imagine. . . . who gives us Christmas every moment.

Dietrich Bonhoffer, in *Letters and Papers from Prison,* wrote this about death:

> Come now, thou greatest of feasts on the journey to freedom eternal; death, cast aside all the burdensome chains, and demolish the walls of our temporal body, the walls of our souls that are blinded, so that at last we may see that which here remains hidden. (371)

If death is the "greatest of feasts"—if all eleven of my relatives are unleashed from pain, ecstatic in spirit, jubilantly soaking up God's love in a great heavenly beach party—then what is grief all about? Why wasn't my first response to any of the deaths, *Hooray for them! Freed at last!*

Many reasons. Because we miss them. Because there is a hole in our lives. Also, someone once said that the greatest part of grief is regret. Regret includes sorrow and remorse, and has to do with unfinished business this side of the grave. Since those of us still living on earth cannot experience Paradise except in brief glints, part of our task after someone we love dies is to clean up the regrets. Because regret is a many-pronged thing (remorse over something we did or didn't do, sorrow that time with the loved one was cut short, regret that the dying one suffered), the main component of regret, as well as the ticket for working through it, is forgiveness. For us who are left behind, we must forgive others for the circumstances of the death, forgive the loved one for leaving us, and forgive ourselves for an imperfect relationship with the one who died.

Forgiving the Circumstances of Death

The Kerrville tragedy forced me to view forgiveness of murderers in a dramatic way, but there are many other ways life can be stolen, sometimes by sheer negligence. People who rob others of life are not always violent, or obvious, or intentionally cruel. People die all the time from the careless behavior of others. My aunt Susan, Juliana's sister, was killed fifteen years ago by a drunk kid who ran a stop sign. Her husband forgave the youth, but my grandmother could not, remaining bitter until the end of her days.

As another example, three years ago, a friend's brother never regained consciousness after surgery. A question arose as to whether the doctor's knife had slipped during the operation. Though the mistake was never proved, still the question festered underneath the words of comfort the family gave each other. Because we live in a fallen world, and because we are inextricably linked to one another in a web of sinfulness, the actions of one are not isolated. What we do has a direct bearing on the lives— and deaths—of others.

This principle branches into greater subtleties. For instance, a man dies at sixty of a heart attack. His brother grieves, blaming the in-laws, claiming they had worked him to death in the family business.

Or, a man marries a young woman after her previous husband has treated her cruelly. The former husband pesters her, stalks her, won't leave her alone; she develops cancer and dies. The husband feels that the former husband's behavior "killed her."

Or, a person dies of AIDS, infected by someone aware, or unaware, of passing on the disease.

Almost nobody dies in a vacuum. All the literature on death says one of the first things we do is look for a repository for the anger we feel at the loss. I remember so well bristling helplessly time and time again, as loved ones were lowered into graves all over the country. Because it is "not acceptable" to rail at God for allowing the tragedy to happen, we seek, like a swollen river, acceptable avenues through which to pour out our anger.

Because grief is a time of confusion and pain, the channels often overflow on the surrounding countryside. For instance, a man who cannot deal with his father's death becomes angry with his wife over irrelevant things. A man blasts the doctor for not allowing experimental drugs to be used on his dying wife. Sooner or later, with guidance and prayer, the flood waters recede and the course of the grieving process moves on. Focusing on side issues, real as they may seem, only keeps grief at the flood stage.

There are no shortcuts. Spiritually, the process is painstaking, and involves reliving much pain and anger. Actually, anger at God is not such an unhealthy thing. Though we know God is not to blame for any death, so many times it seems that He turns a blind eye by allowing His permissive will to occur. He stands dead-center when we are looking for a target. I'm convinced that God loves us so much that He is willing to take the blame, to absorb our anger, when we need a punching bag. I think He would rather have us yelling at Him than not speaking at all. Again, the psalmist gives us an example of how to deal with both God and our enemies—those we perceive as having caused or participated in the death of someone we love. Jesus Himself echoed the psalmist in His hour of desperation, "My God, my God, why hast thou forsaken me?" (Matthew 27:46). Sagging from the cross, He cried in anguish, anger, incomprehension, reproach. "Where were You when I needed You?" Yet it is a cry that keeps the dialogue open.

If we keep the channels open, if we continue to ask for the ability to forgive, we will receive it. The problem is getting to the place where we want to ask for it. Too many reasons not to forgive get in the way. The person isn't sorry, the crime was too obscene, we want the person to hurt as much as we do. Time is the key, allowing the Holy Spirit to soothe the wounds gently.

In the case of my aunt, uncle, and cousin, my prayers went something like this:

Lord, I am so angry that You allowed these young men to walk in and kill my family. I'm angry that they had to die so brutally.

Lord, please help me to be not so mad at You. Please help me stop hating the two men.

Lord, I can't forgive these people, I simply can't.

Lord, please don't ask me to do something I can't do.

Lord, I'm sorry.

Lord, I know I should forgive these two men. You told us to forgive our enemies. But surely You didn't mean people this wicked, who do things this evil.

Lord, thank You for giving me the power to do something I can't do on my own.

Lord, all right. I can't forgive these people yet, but if You give me the grace to work on it, I will.

Lord, please give me more grace, because I still hate these men.

Lord, please show Yourself to these men. Please let Your light shine in their faces. I know You forgive them.

Lord, thank You for loving us more than we can imagine.

The prayer does not end here. I will continue the dialogue for a long time, not resting on my own desire to forgive these men, but in God's grace to change my heart.

Regretting the circumstances of death, even murder, is to focus on the wrong issue. The loved ones are in the hands of a loving God; they are saying joyously, "Oh, I understand now, I get it!" while we are bogged down in the mire of anger and non-understanding. Yet the only way we, too, get a glimmer of the peace that passes understanding is to finish the work of regret. We must forgive those involved in a loved one's death.

Forgiving the Person Who Died

Years ago, I read that it is important to forgive the person who died for dying. *Sure,* I thought at the time. *Maybe in the case of a suicide, or self-abuse, or an overdose. But otherwise, why should I need to forgive a person for something they can't help?* That statement made no sense to me until so many people I loved actually died.

My grandmother's body lay wilting and wasting away in a nursing home for several years before her strong heart finally petered out. At ninety-seven, she was finally released by death. However, most of our family's recent deaths were not so timely, or so welcome. My brother-in-law Tom and my cousin Adrienne, both in their early forties, were forced to abandon unfinished business, leaving the rest of us speechless on this side of Jordan's bank, embracing air and memories. *How could they do this?*

A good example is this story. In their early thirties, John and Marilyn were happily married and in the thick of raising three teenagers, when the lump in Marilyn's breast turned out to be cancer. John had grown up in a home where his alcoholic mother had dropped out of the family emotionally when he was still in grade school, running around on his father, and had taken off permanently when John was in college. As a result, John had developed serious issues of abandonment, especially by women.

Before Marilyn met John, in her former marriage, she had come home from work one evening and found herself marooned in an empty house. Without notice, her husband had walked out. When Marilyn met John, their respective needs for security collided and they fell in love. It was a perfect match.

Until Marilyn died. Choked up, John said, "I know it's irrational, but I'm so mad at Marilyn. She left me after all." His worst fear had been realized, and he felt abandoned.

John's minister helped him work through his anger at Marilyn, and he realized his feelings had more to do with his own baggage than with her death. He was able to forgive her, and began healing from his past traumas, which had caused the anger in the first place.

He also realized that though Marilyn may have "abandoned" him, God had not.

Another example is Mrs. Thomason. In the insurance business, Mr. Thomason, seventy-two, had died suddenly at his desk of a stroke. Until he died, his widow didn't know his business was going bankrupt; nor did she know that he did not leave her any life insurance. As a friend commented sadly, "The cobbler's family has no shoes." Mrs. Thomason, seventy-one, was left penniless through her husband's negligence.

Angry? Depressed? Yes, and Mrs. Thomason bore these feelings along with her sadness. Her grief work was complicated because of the circumstances. She discovered the difficult paradox of longing for someone you miss, and being simultaneously furious at him.

The week after my brother-in-law Tom's funeral, I opened the weekly bulletin from the church where Tom and my sister had been co-ministers. However, instead of finding his usual column of witty, pungent advice on spiritual matters, an empty half-page square of white glared at me. In the center, the church secretary had typed Tom's name and the dates of his life span. I threw the church bulletin across the room. *How could Tom leave my sister and the kids like this? How could he deprive my children of a beloved uncle? How could he leave me too?* I needed my brother badly, to hear what he would say about how to handle this loss. *And he wasn't there to help any of us.*

Astonished at the irrationality of my feelings, the anger eventually distilled into a pool of sadness. As I prayed for Tom, I remembered that as a Presbyterian, he had questioned our Episcopal prayer for the departed: "We commend to Your mercy all those who have died, that Your will for them may be fulfilled." Crumpled on the couch among the scattered mail, I realized why we pray for the dead, besides the theological reasons. For comfort. To picture them in the arms of God. So that we might understand them better. As I prayed for Tom, I began to know him in a more profound way than I had when he was alive. I was able to see more clearly what his life was about. After I had confessed that I was mad at Tom for leaving, God opened my eyes to the treasure heap of blessings Tom had piled up around my sister and the children and all of us.

The Timing of Death

In one of my dark times, Tom had once related C. S. Lewis' image of the slender beam of light from another world shining into the dark shed of our earthly understanding. Almost as an extension of that conversation, Tom bequeathed to me a different peek through a knothole into *kairos.* I could almost hear his slow, measured voice interpreting a realm I didn't understand into a realm

I do. "In chronological terms, the timing doesn't seem fair, but God's in charge. His timing is measured by instruments we don't have. It's okay."

Only in a limited sense can we pick the best time and way to go. Tom made up his mind he would make it through the Christmas season. Already a skeleton, he suffered anew when brain tumors exploded Christmas morning as he was unwrapping gifts under the tree. Yet he hung on, determined. His was a testament to the human spirit: He made it, dying finally on the Epiphany. If he could have, I know he'd have hung on for the next twenty years, to walk his daughters down the aisle, to continue teaching, to enjoy his marriage, to live.

God's timing is not our timing. But it's okay. It has to be.

Forgiving Ourselves

Forgiveness. The net widens. We must forgive those involved in the death and the one who died, but often the hardest person to forgive is ourselves. My cousin Adrienne had made a disparaging remark about the Christmas card I sent her the Christmas before she was killed. On green paper, I had Xeroxed my children's illustrations of lopsided Christmas trees and startling, bat-like angels. Adrienne had made fun of the card, saying to my mother, "Well, Leslie must be low on funds this year." What she said hurt my feelings, not only because I *was* low on funds, but because I had found my children's pictures delightful and irresistible, and she clearly did not.

After she died, I recalled her comment, and the resentment I had harbored against her. I also remembered how I had hurt her feelings by not calling her myself when our daughter Caroline arrived; my mother had called Juliana, and Adrienne had heard the news from her mother. Suddenly, small memories from over the years began to sting me, stinging and stinging—the little slights, the petty trafficking between cousins close in age, beginning with the party she got to go to and I didn't that summer I was four and she was seven. Twenty years later, she had taken me in as a roommate in San Antonio, and I had never told her how much her kindness meant to me.

Adrienne and I had not finished our kinship or our friendship, and I had to inventory the relationship one-sidedly, forgiving both Adrienne and myself for forty years of being human.

Interestingly, the word *remorse* contains the prefix "re," meaning "again," and the root for "sting," "bite," and "attack." These stinging regrets swarmed inside my soul after every family member's death except my grandmother's. With Mamah, I had said good-bye, and cleaned out the attic. But the others—why hadn't I written to Uncle Windy more often? Why didn't I tell Jerre how much he had meant to me?

Regrets over Tom's death were the deepest. Tom lived with us off and on for nine months when we first moved to Houston, during one of the most difficult periods of my life, as I've described before. We'd been hit financially, emotionally, physically. For me, these culminated in an acute case of asthma, as our chaotic household headed into a Christmas both frantic and depressing.

By the end of November, I felt close to a physical and emotional breaking point. The most difficult thing was listening to Tom's racking cough, wondering whether he would die in his sleep, which was a very real possibility. Also, I did not deal well with his depression. I kept encouraging him to get help, suggesting all the things I would have done, not considering that he was different in temperament and nature. I kept pushing him toward life, sensing that he was allowing himself to drown.

As the pandemonium of Christmas clattered closer, I wheezedly told Tom I didn't know if I could handle his staying with us through the first part of December. I knew he'd had other offers of places to stay with friends and other relatives, but he'd always stayed with us. And I'd been glad to have him.

He was devastated. I had wounded him in a way I didn't understand, and at a time when he was more vulnerable than I could imagine. I wrote him a letter, apologizing for my weakness, trying to make him feel welcome once again in our home. Because he was a kind and loving man, he forgave me.

A year later, he was gone.

Only in retrospect did I see that I had failed him in another, deeper way. When he was with us, I had expended much of my emotional energy trying to pour life back into Tom, trying to force him into living, when what he needed was someone to help him die, to give him permission to leave.

Asking God for help in forgiving myself for failing Tom has been a repeated prayer request. Each time I struggle with it, I gain a more profound sense of what God tries to tell us about forgiveness and love—how the intersections of peoples' needs can cause pain, how imperfectly and selfishly we try to give to each other, and yet how love transcends all our paltry attempts to be useful. Tom has forgiven me, God has forgiven me. When I finally forgave myself, instead of focusing on my own shortcomings, I became free instead to remember Tom more clearly, and to give thanks for his humor, his wisdom, his presence, his brilliance, his love that he gave us when he walked among us.

Prerequisites and Results of Forgiveness

In the Gospels, God's forgiveness of us is linked to two other conditions—one a prerequisite (our forgiveness of other people), and the other a result (healing). In the Lord's Prayer, forgiveness is a package deal: God forgives us *as we forgive others.* Because

Jesus taught us to pray like this, I take the issue of forgiveness to be more than just a good suggestion. It is a matter of life and death. Ours.

The acid of unforgiveness eventually eats away, not the person who has done the damage, but the one who can't forgive. If I lie awake at night raging against my family's murderers, who gets destroyed? Them? They don't even know I exist. No, I do. I suffer the double-whammy of damage to myself over something I can never change, and also the selfimposed separation between God and me. God cannot come near a cauldron of anger. He cannot soothe me if I am consumed with unforgiveness.

In addition, hating the murderers until I die gives them power over me for the rest of my life. Do I want to give such people that kind of power? No, of course not. Therefore, for all these reasons, both holy and selfish, I pray to God for the grace to forgive the criminals. In the process, I know that my own sins will be forgiven.

In the Gospels, forgiveness is directly linked to healing. In Matthew, Mark, and Luke, the story is told of the paralytic brought to Jesus by his friends, who lower him on a pallet through the roof. Impressed with the faith of the friends, Jesus says first to the man, "My son, your sins are forgiven." When He senses the spirit of the scribes accusing Him of blasphemy, He asks them whether it is easier to forgive sins or to heal. He follows the more difficult task of forgiveness with healing: "rise, take up your pallet and go home" (Mark 2:5–11), proving His authority on earth. Forgiveness first, then healing.

Not surprisingly for us, too, true healing of the spirit and of memories comes after the more difficult work of forgiveness.

The problem with death is that it seems so final. The news of each family member's death felt like an abrupt silence on the other end of a phone conversation. The dialogue became a monologue before I was ready to stop communicating. Yet I found out how important it is to finish our end of the conversation, even when the other party can no longer respond. Asking God for the power of forgiveness—of those dealing with the death, of the loved one, and of ourselves—restores and cleans the memory of the relationship and sanctifies it in our hearts. Blessed are those who have the chance to do the work of forgiveness before death severs the relationship. Blessed, too, is the one who dies.

In literature, one of the most powerful stories ever written about dying is Tolstoy's "The Death of Ivan Ilych," a short piece that should be required reading for anyone with a family member in the last stages of a disease. Through Ivan's eyes, we experience what it's like to move from a comfortable life to the brink of the grave. We sigh and cringe at relatives who don't know how to respond. We review our lives as Ivan reviews his, culling meaning from the bridge games, the redecorating, the shallow parties he'd been consumed with.

The climax of the story occurs when Ivan realizes that he needs to tell his family he's sorry for the way he's lived. "He tried to add, 'forgive me,' but said, 'forgo' and waved his hand"; however, Ivan knew that "He [God] whose understanding mattered would understand." This crucial act accomplished, he makes his final, stunning revelation:

> There was no fear because there was no death. In place of death there was light. "So that's what it is!" he suddenly exclaimed aloud. "What joy!" (1263)

No matter what the circumstances, God always has the last word. Always. And it is a word of triumph. There is no death! What joy! For those of us still left on earth puzzling it out, ultimately, after weeping through the night, we notice that the shades lighten slowly, and sunlight eventually pours in, making the dust motes dance, and making the room habitable once again.

The peace of God passes understanding.

As for me, I know that my Redeemer lives
and that at the last he will stand upon the earth.
After my awaking, he will raise me up;
and in my body I shall see God.
I myself shall see, and my eyes behold him
who is my friend and not a stranger . . . .

Happy from now on
are those who die in the Lord!
So it is, says the Spirit,
for they rest from their labors.

(THE BOOK OF COMMON PRAYER, *page 469*)

9

The Peace that Passes Understanding

I lie down in peace; at once I fall asleep; for only you,
Lord, make me dwell in safety.
—*Psalm 4*, THE BOOK OF COMMON PRAYER

Tommy's father's blue velveteen bathrobe trailed behind him down the aisle, and his gold spray-painted crown had slipped over one ear. His little sister Elise belted out, "We Three Kings of Orien Tar," as Tommy gingerly carried the homemade jewel-studded cigar box to the Baby Jesus at the front of the church. Tommy's two friends waited up near the manger already, Jake shuffling his tennis shoes peeking out from beneath a fake-ermine costume, and Patrick grasping one of his mother's perfume bottles with one hand and picking his nose with the other. When Tommy reached the front, Elise whispered to her mother, "Look at the presents for the Baby Jesus! Gold, circumstance, and mud!"

I have always loved this rendition of the Wise Men story, though I'm not sure where the story came from. Elise's description of the gifts seems to me in many ways more truly symbolic of what we actually bring before the Lord. Like the Wise Men, we travel on a spiritual journey seeking Christ, and when we find Him, we give Him the only thing we have to offer—our lives. We surrender our gold, yes—we pledge to the church, or drop our change in the plate on Sunday. We also give Him nuggets of what we hold most dear, the shining treasures He has given us in the first place: our loved ones with their endearing or eccentric habits; our children, with their smudged faces, their twenty million questions, and their sudden hugs; our talents, both polished and squandered; our brains; our personalities; our love—impulsive, shy, conditional.

We also present to Him our circumstances—the crazy, happy, disappointing events of our lives, the coincidences, the discoveries, the slow maturation of our faith. And finally, we give to Jesus our mud—those trials we slog through, the bogs of despair, misunderstanding, sadness, grief.

If we love Christ with all our hearts, we give Him not foreign, exotic goods like myrrh, but the real stuff of our lives: gold, circumstance, and mud.

Another reason I like this rendition is because mud is what we are during the hard times: dust and tears. Of all the gifts we give to the Baby Jesus, mud may be the most sincere.

In some Christian circles, the illusion hovers over certain testimonies that if you give your life to Jesus, your problems go away. Stockton and I have heard people witness to this, describing first their worldly despair followed by the miracle: "My business was bankrupt and I was miserable until I invited Jesus into my life. Then, presto! I met a wonderful blonde who became my wife and I made a bunch of money." We call this the "Mercedes gospel."

I'm not about to deny these experiences. God works in every way possible, including the miraculous. However, most people I know do not experience the evaporation of their problems after accepting Christ. In the Old Testament, after being freed from their bondage in Egypt, the Israelites found themselves not in the Promised Land, but in the desert for forty years. In fact, many new Christians find themselves not with a Mercedes and a blonde, but flat on their faces in the mud with questions, quandaries, issues they never knew existed before.

For those of us who feel guilty that our problems multiplied in complexity instead of disappearing when we became Christians, there is still hope! God is not a vending machine for Christians dispensing what we think we need. The Christian journey is instead the process of learning to accept Christ's outstretched hand as He leads us down the sometimes mucky road of life. We may be covered with slosh from struggling along—but once we get to the top of the hill, the vistas are breathtaking.

If we pretend not to dirty ourselves with the real entanglements of life, then we put ourselves above Jesus. Jesus faced genuine temptation in the desert; He also struggled with loss, betrayal, disappointment—everything we wrestle with. Though He did not sin, He knew firsthand the agony of the human condition. The Word became flesh . . . clay . . . mud. Mud has been sanctified because God stooped to become one of us, to know us inside out.

In John 9:6–9, Jesus spits on the ground, makes mud, and places the mud on a blind man's eyes. He tells the man to go wash it off in the pool of Siloam. When he does as Jesus asks, the blind man walks away, his sight restored. In this miracle, mud was the means used by Christ for healing. We should not disdain the mud of our lives: Out of the mud spring miracles.

Peace in the Bible

As I have lain on my couch in the night, wrestling with different issues, I have often "chased after the Mercedes," so to speak, asking for God's material, measurable blessings in my life. I have begged God for children, for healing for loved ones, for a church filled with love instead of backbiting, for a job, for a new town, for a verdict of justice in the court system. Some of my requests have been granted—later or sooner. However, as I look back over those many years of dark nights, the most astonishing gift God has given me is the gift of peace, which comes with the awareness of His presence.

Let me play around here for a minute with the idea of peace. In the Bible, beginning in Genesis and winding through the New Testament, the idea of peace evolves from something material to something spiritual. There is a definable shift in meaning between the testaments with the coming of Christ. In the beginning, "peace" meant happiness in all aspects. *Shalom* has many broad uses. First, in Genesis 29:6, Jacob arrives in Laban's land. He asks Laban's friends how things are going with his Uncle Laban. "It is well," they reply. *Shalom* here means "fine." Second, in 1 Kings 3:1 and 9:25, Solomon has finished his house and the temple. Used here, the word *Shalom* implies "completion." Third, in Proverbs 3:2, "peace" means "abundant welfare"; fourth, in Isaiah 41:3, it means "safety." Finally, in 2 Kings, the word *shalom* means "success in war," or "victory."

In the Old Testament, then, peace meant everything from assurance of prosperity (cows, land), to protection from enemies. The old covenant dealt with a material peace in the promised land. Peace was strongly tied to victory over invading enemies; peace meant the absence of war, with the Israelites in control.

With the new covenant, though, the idea of peace shifted from tangible, earthly welfare to spiritual welfare, just as the new covenant emphasized the kingdom within, not a kingdom on earth. The new covenant with God did not include assurance of good health, plenty of livestock, no fighting with neighbors. The new covenant promised something even more exciting.

When the risen Christ greets the apostles, He says, "Peace be with you" (John 20:19). Jesus has replaced David as king. David was sent by God to protect the chosen people, to ensure peace against the enemies of the promised land, and the risen Christ has now ushered in a new reign of a different kind of peace. Jesus is the Dispenser of a peace that passes understanding, that cannot be measured in wealth or health or prosperity or lack of war. This new kind of peace is a gift we can carry with us, no matter what our circumstances are. This kind of peace exists along with *and transcends* wars and physical trials. "I have said this to you, that in me you may have peace. In the world you have tribulation; but be of good cheer, I have overcome the world" (John 16:33).

So what does this actually mean as we're trekking down the road, like Christian in *Pilgrim's Progress,* stuck in the Slough of Despondency or flitting through Vanity Fair? In real terms, what does this "peace that passeth understanding" mean to us as we are wrestling in the dark on our couches?

Peace as Protection

First, God's peace is protection. The world really isn't a nice place. The world is dangerous. We Christians get caught in wars, robberies, disease, starvation, and drive-by shootings, just like the rest of humanity. God's peace doesn't guarantee we won't be touched by the world. No. Jesus assured us we *will* be knocked around by evils the world inflicts on its inhabitants. Rather, God's peace is like an inner lining to keep the world's fears and destruction from eating and destroying our souls.

Medical procedures terrify me, and several years ago I faced a painful procedure, with no medication provided. Before I went into the doctor's office, I prayed for protection from fear and pain. I remember lying on that cold table in a skimpy, backless gown, breathing deeply, trying not to hyperventilate as the doctor approached with the instruments. I closed my eyes and prayed for the presence of the Holy Spirit to infiltrate my body.

My prayer was answered. I walked away peaceful, having withstood the pain with grace. God did not take away the problem, nor the pain. However, He did give me the protection of His peace. This has not always been the case—due to my own negligence and faithlessness, not God's. When I remember to pray for the presence of God in times of trial, this prayer is honored, and peace seems to flow in my bloodstream, washing through my very cells. When I forget to pray for protection, allowing fear to swarm and pain to prick, the experience is always more traumatic.

At the end of Charles Dickens' *A Tale of Two Cities,* Sidney Carton dies in the place of Charles Darnay—not for Darnay's sake, but because he loves Darnay's wife so much, he is willing to sacrifice his life to make her happy with her husband. As the tumbrels rumble through the streets of Paris, heading toward the guillotine, Carton gives another prisoner—an innocent, young woman—strength and courage to face her grisly death right before his. Then, when it is his turn, Carton quotes scripture: "I am the resurrection and the life, saith the Lord: he that believeth in me, though he were dead, yet shall he live: and whosoever liveth and believeth in me, shall never die!"

The result of his faith is the response on his face right before he is beheaded: "They said of him, about the city that night, that it was the peacefulest man's face ever beheld there" (417). In the greatest trial of all, facing death, Carton's conviction of faith gave him the peace that passed understanding. Further, the power of this peace was not merely a gift to Carton, but became a gift shared with others around him. The young prisoner he kissed right before her death was affected by his peace, as were the spectators, lined up grimly knitting. This peace was so remarkable that news of it was passed around a city steeped in blood and fear.

Oswald Chambers describes the Christian in relation to the difficulties of the world:

> An average view of the Christian life is that it means deliverance from trouble. It is deliverance *in* trouble, which is very different. . . . If you are a child of God, there certainly will be troubles to meet, but Jesus says do not be surprised when they come. . . . God does not give us overcoming life: He gives us life as we overcome. (215)

God's peace is inner protection against the evils of the world. Evil may pierce the body, but doesn't have to destroy the soul.

Peace as Divine Integration

God's peace is the divine integration of all the many parts of our personhood. We humans are hardly simple creatures. Our lives are a continual balancing act: Instinct is played against reason, spirituality against flesh. We are called on to integrate our pasts into the present—not a simple task. The events on our calendars are played out daily, and the roles we select are influenced by our perception of reality, our subconscious, our personality, our health.

I think of the totality of our being as divided into segments. One segment is our past; another is our ego, our personality; another is our unconscious; another is our daily list of things to do; another is our spiritual life, our connection to the divine. All these factors make up who we are. However, the segments are not always in the correct proportion. Sometimes the ego is extra-large.

Sometimes the daily list of things to do takes over the whole, and squeezes the spiritual segment to a sliver.

Another way of looking at the mix of the parts of ourselves is to picture the facets of our personalities as ingredients of a pie, dumped in a bowl in what we hope are pleasing proportions, but maybe not. Maybe our subconscious is so heavy with unworked-through material, it clogs the recipe with too much flour. Our hopes and dreams and egos are tossed in a bowl and stirred by life, and sometimes that's exactly what it feels like—being tossed and stirred by life. But in order to become a real pie, we need to be stirred. We also need to be cooked, and God's love in this analogy is like the heat necessary for us to blend together into the person God wants us to become. If God did not allow life to stir us up, and if He did not allow us to "feel the heat," we would remain a lumpy mass of disparate ingredients. God's love is the catalyst to change raw materials into a delectable treat.

The peace that passes understanding, then, is what we feel when we're being lifted gingerly, carefully out of the oven, displayed as a masterpiece. We have become whole. The ingredients of our lives have become integrated. Only then are we ready to be used to feed others.

When, by prayer, grace, discipline, our lives have reached a delicate balance, this precarious state of our souls, psyches, personalities, and needs never seems to last nearly as long as I'd like. It seems that, just as I've worked through one thing, something else occurs to disrupt the balance. I used to fight the disruptions, seeking the elusive peace balance brings. Now I try to accept the new disruption, knowing that the extremes of existence, though keeping me off-balance, also keep me off-center, placing God in the control seat, where He belongs. Disruption, like failure, is an opportunity for spiritual growth.

The Price of Peace

As we all know, God's peace is not gained easily. Jesus paid dearly for the gift of peace, hanging on the cross for us sinners. We don't deserve peace at all; rather, we deserve the trials we inflict on ourselves and others through our sin and ignorance. However, God paid so we could share in the gift of peace, and part of our gratitude is remembering the cost of Jesus' suffering.

For us, too, peace also does not come cheaply. Like grace, peace is free, but expensive. We earn it through suffering. We earn it by dying to ourselves and our selfish desires. We earn it through wrestling tough issues to the ground, thrashing until dawn through the long, dark night of the soul. We earn it, only to realize that we didn't earn it at all. It is a gift. The peace that passes understanding is one of the great paradoxes of the faith. It is free, but not easy to come by.

In addition, the peace that passes understanding is more than the absence of strife or conflict. It is not dead air. It is not an empty house. The peace that passes understanding is a creative state of being fulfilled and filled, not with self, but with God. This is infinitely better than getting our heart's desire. As both Oscar Wilde and G. B. Shaw said, there are two tragedies in life: One is not to get one's heart's desire, and the other is to get it. The peace that passes understanding bypasses the heart's desire entirely, giving us not what we thought we wanted, but what God wanted us to have—which turns out to be better than anything our puny imaginations could concoct in the first place.

Many years ago, when I first saw the movie *Fantasia,* the last scene, "Good versus Evil," fascinated me. "Evil" was represented visually in alluring, vivid colors and startling movement, accompanied by music challenging to the senses. "Good" was represented by a peaceful woods, a monochromatic, motionless scene with music that seemed blah after evil's racing beat.

The peace of "good" bored my socks off.

The *Fantasia* experience confirmed a deep, unspoken fear that heaven might not be all that it's cracked up to be in the way of holding my interest.

I was younger then. Yet even at the time, I thought, *This can't be right.* If we acted the way we were created to act, true good and true peace would be every bit as captivating and fulfilling as evil's empty promises. Now, after many years, I know that in Christ, true peace is by far more alluring than anything the world dangles in front of us. True peace is a soul-tingling, bell-ringing peal of an experience. It's not just a vague quietude you get when you hear the birds sing. No. Peace is an inner festival.

Finally, peace is directly related to love. Frederick Buechner describes this relationship in *Wishful Thinking*. He says that Jesus' title, the Prince of Peace, seems to be contradictory at first. One time Jesus says to the disciples, "Do not think that I have come to bring peace on earth; I have not come to bring peace, but a sword" (Matthew 10:34). Then, later, Jesus tells them, "Peace I leave with you; my peace I give to you" (John 14:27). Buechner concludes: "The contradiction is resolved when you realize that for Jesus peace seems to have meant not the absence of struggle but the presence of love" (69).

As any parent knows, the process of telling a child s/he is loved involves anger-producing denial of requests. Love means not letting the toddler stick her finger in the light socket no matter how much she is determined to do it, no matter how red-faced and loud the angry response. If love is defined as an act rather than the sentimental feeling we get when we look at a sleeping child, we understand Jesus' comments more clearly. Jesus did not write a series of sonnets entitled, "How I Love the Human Race." He did not write romantic music in our honor. No, instead He crawled up on the cross and died. He acted because He loved us.

God's peace is a direct result of God's love for us. Peace is not the tranquillity felt when gazing at a pastoral landscape. Peace is the view from the cross. Peace follows struggle with a God who loves us and sometimes acts in ways we rebel against. Jesus bought peace for a great price, and so do we.

Peace Defined

Peace needs to be distinguished from other words with similar connotations. Peace, for instance, is not the same thing as joy. As C. S. Lewis defines it in *Surprised by Joy,* joy is a quickening, a "quivering in the diaphragm" from desire; it is a stab of yearning to be a part of God. Joy enters into our daily experience, mostly when our attention is focused on something besides itself; joy is an inkling of the divine we experience as longing for God (219).

Happiness, as distinct from peace, is linked with its root word, "hap" which means "luck." The pleasing sensation we experience when we are lucky, when things are going our way, depends on our outward circumstances. We get money back from the IRS and we are happy; we owe money in April and we are not. Pleasure, too, is distinct from peace because pleasure is often within our control and results from achieving something we seek. We experience pleasure in many things, from biting into a juicy orange to buying a yacht. Pleasure results in something we do. Finally, gladness, as my mother once pointed out, is distinct from joy in that it implies endurance, a willingness to go forward without necessarily the thrill or ecstasy of desire. In one of the Episcopal closing communion prayers, we go forth to love and serve Christ "with gladness and singleness of heart" (365).

These four words differ from peace. Peace is the relief after intense struggle. Peace is the knitting together of the loose and dangerous strands of our pain. Peace is deep trust in God, gained after He has wrestled us to the ground. Horatio J. Spafford in the last century defined peace after he watched his entire family drown at sea in a disastrous storm that wrecked the ship they traveled in. As a result of the accident, he was left alone in the world. After witnessing the tragedy, he wrote the beautiful hymn, "It Is Well with My Soul."

It is well with my soul. That is the peace that passes understanding.

Peace Not of the Earth

God's peace is something not of this earth, and occurs in our lives in about the same proportion as Raskolnikov's experience in *Crime and Punishment*. Dostoevsky spends 477 pages on Raskolnikov's inner turmoil, suffering, anguish, violence, evil, and discord, and just fourteen pages describing the peace of God he achieves at the end. The glimpses of peace we receive now are rare, wonderful, treasured moments, tiny hors d'oevres of the feast to come. Being creatures of the world as well as spiritual beings tagged for heaven, we experience unpeace more than peace. The many wicked facets of unpeace—unforgiveness, war, envy, fear, lust (the list seems, unfortunately, endless)—grab our attention. Like the news media, capitalizing on rapes, murders, drug deals, and car wrecks, the results of unpeace are thrust in the forefront of our attention. Peace and love do not sell copy because part of our nature thrives on the presence of their opposites. The problem, of course, is sin. It is only through the grace of Jesus Christ that we experience real peace at all.

Because we so often settle for less, I sometimes wonder about our capacity—fallen creatures that we are—to stand peace for any length of time. True peace is a sweetness, something too rich, perhaps, for our digestive systems now. True peace is like seeing Christ face to face: an experience so moving, so awesome, so terrifying in a way that I'm not sure, on this earth, we can stand more than the fleeting glimpses we receive.

My experience, however, is that peace is worth praying for every minute of every day. The struggle is always worth it: God's peace makes holy our relationships with others, with ourselves, and with the Almighty.

How Jacob Found Peace

Jacob spent the long night in the desert wrestling with God not in mud, but in sand. Still, the experience must have been gritty, difficult. Many years earlier, on his way to Haran to find a wife, he had also spent the night under the stars, with a rock for a pillow. That was the night of his magnificent vision in a dream, of a ladder ascending to heaven, with angels going up and down. The Lord stood above the ladder, and made Jacob a mighty promise:

> The land on which you lie I will give to you and to your
> descendants; and your descendants shall be like the dust of
> the earth, and you shall spread abroad to the west and to the
> east and to the north and to the south; and by you and your
> descendants shall all the families of the earth bless them-
> selves. (Genesis 28:14)

For a young kid just getting started in life, this is heady stuff. God's message was also the opposite of the chastisement Jacob might have expected to hear, after he'd just robbed his older brother of both birthright and blessing. So Jacob had reason to be doubly pleased.

Jacob's response to the dream is two-fold. First, he is properly respectful: "How awesome is this place!" (Genesis 28:17). He sets up a pillar with the stone he used as a pillow, and anoints the stone, calling the place *Bethel.* Second, he makes a promise to God: "The Lord shall be my God," vowing to give to God a tenth of all he has. His promise, though, is tempered with a condition—if God will keep him in food and clothes, *"so that I come again to my father's house in peace"* (emphasis mine). Then and only then does he accept God (Genesis 28:20–22).

After the night of the first vision, when Jacob had committed himself to the Lord, he goes on to find Laban, to marry twice, and to head home after many years. Let us compare the first night out on the desert alone with the night before he met Esau, when he was again alone under the stars. Jacob did not receive a beatific vision this time, a promise of a good life and many descendants. He was threatened instead with instant extinction by an unidentified adversary if he did not fight with every sinew.

Jacob was older and wiser than when he started out. Presumably, he was more mature spiritually, and needed at this stage of his development, not a sweet vision, but a toughening experience. Patriarchs, along with the rest of us, did not gain strength and integrity from cushy lives.

The initial experience was a dream—a powerful, evocative vision, but a dream nonetheless. The second experience was God in the flesh, an even more powerful event—the most profound, terrifying, awe-inspiring experience known to living beings. The intensity of communication on God's part had increased.

Jacob attached conditions to both encounters in his response. He committed himself to God in the first instance, provided God did as He promised. The night he wrestled with God, Jacob refused to let go when God asked him to. Even though he'd been wounded in the thigh, he held on until the Being had blessed him.

What We Learn Through Jacob

What does Jacob's experience say to us? Many times we, too, at first receive a gentler vision. We encounter the love and the promises of Jesus, and our hearts are touched, like Jacob's. We know we've been in the presence of the Holy, and we want to make it known. We promise to tithe, we promise to follow Jesus, and our hearts sing for joy.

Then life intervenes. The initial high is hard to maintain. We find our circumstances difficult, even death-threatening, like Jacob, and we find ourselves again on the desert floor, trying to sleep. Only this time, we don't get a nice, comforting dream. Instead, we are waked by a Being who pounces on us, a Being we do not recognize at first. We know it is a fight to the death but we think it is an adversary, someone working at trying to kill us, because our opponent is so strong and so serious about the match.

We realize as we struggle that we, like Jacob, have put strings on the relationship from the first—conditions, probably unconscious, that have not been fulfilled. "Oh, Lord, I will love You if You promise to take care of me. If You give me food and clothes (or children, or a steady income, or a spouse, or health)." Because these conditions have not been met, just as Jacob's promises were threatened that night with annihilation the next day, we find ourselves alone in the dark, struggling.

We discover that we have to give over our lives again to God. We are struggling for power, for control of our destiny. As each new part of our life develops and is threatened, we have to wrestle over and over and over, giving up more and more of ourselves until God has as much of us as we can give Him. As with Jacob, this is a fight to the death. Our opponent is serious, and so are we.

Wrestling is a toughening experience, and one that changes us from beginners to veterans in the faith. However, we are being toughened not so we will be destroyed, but so that we will be blessed even more richly than before. Though we, like Jacob, walk with a limp from the experience, the blessing makes up for the pain.

The night Jacob wrestled with God, he had other things to deal with too. He couldn't run away from his past forever. In his case, facing his past meant risking not just his life, but the lives of his family and household as well.

Because Jacob was willing to deal effectively with his past, his future also fell into place. He did not let his terror of what might happen to him stop him from doing what he needed to do. In this way, he fulfilled God's plan for his life, and we are still reaping the blessings today for his faithfulness.

We, too, must face our pasts, no matter who has hurt us or what we've done to hurt others. We, too, have destinies in Christ, and cannot afford to be crippled by unresolved problems or by fear of what's to come. Like Jacob, we must trust that the promises of God will be fulfilled.

As Jacob rolled around in the sand, grappling in the dark, he realized that his arms embraced, not a spirit or an imagined foe, but a physical Being of blood and flesh. The mystery of a spiritual God who becomes flesh leads us to examine the relationship between spirit and matter in our own lives. Though we live in a culture obsessed by materialism, and though our fleshly bodies intercept and decode the reality around us, the focus of our lives is necessarily spiritual, if we believe in God incarnate in Christ. We are both our souls and bodies; we are not merely souls trapped in bodies because God does something wonderful, miraculous, and unexplainable with our bodies when we die. If God can become flesh first in the desert with Jacob, and later in Christ, then the message becomes clear. Both our spirits and our bodies have value in God's eyes, and the spiritual quest involves seeking to understand the spirit/matter relationship on a cellular, day-to-day, and cultural level.

Jacob wrestles with God alone. He has no audience; he has no cheering section; he has no helpers. Under the great black sky, the struggle is between him and God and nobody else. This is the great truth for all of us: We come to know God in our most intense moments alone. God gives us community, as God surrounded Jacob with his family and his household, and they may have been praying for him across the river. For us, the church is where we seek strength in worshipping together. Yet the great moments of insight, conviction, and power take place between us and God, alone. By cultivating the garden of solitude with Jesus, we find solitude even in a crowd and can turn loneliness into strength. We also begin on earth the lifelong relationship that truly blossoms when we die.

Jacob is blessed by God and given a new name. He lives many years in peace with a new identity. We, too, are given a new identity after we've wrestled through the night with God. We limp from the experience but the blessing of peace, even if it's only a short-lived glimpse of Paradise, is worth the pain. Our time of trouble on earth is short. Eternity lies ahead, and we will no longer wrestle in the darkness but will see our Savior face to face.

In reviewing Jacob's story, we see the many issues that he struggled with, and how his story is our story too. It is only when God has wrestled Jacob to the ground, when God has marked Jacob with a thigh wound, and when Jacob has refused to let go until he's been blessed, that God allows the last part of Jacob's original condition to come to pass: "so that I come again to my father's house in peace" (Genesis 28:21).

Thanks be to God!

O Lord, support us all the day long, until the shadows lengthen, and the evening comes, and the busy world is hushed, and the fever of life is over, and our work is done. Then in your mercy, grant us a safe lodging, and a holy rest, and peace at the last. Amen.

(THE BOOK OF COMMON PRAYER, *page 833*)

Works Cited

A&E. "Biography." December 11, 1995. 8:00 P.M., CST.

Augustine of Hippo. *Confessions.* Trans. R. S. Pine-Coffin. Baltimore, MD: Penguin Books, 1961.

Barber, Wayne. "Course on Romans" tape. Chattanooga, TN: Precepts Ministries.

Bonhoffer, Dietrich. *Letters and Papers from Prison.* The Enlarged Edition. Eberhard Bethge, ed. New York: Macmillan, 1953.

The Book of Common Prayer. The Church Hymnal Corporation and The Seabury Press, 1979.

Buechner, Frederick. *Wishful Thinking.* New York: Harper and Row, 1973.

Buttrick, George Arthur, ed. *Interpreter's Bible.* Vol. 7. New York: Abingdon, 1951.

Carretto, Carlo. *The God Who Comes.* Trans. Rose Mary Hancock. Maryknoll, NY: Orbis Books, 1974.

Chambers, Oswald. *My Utmost for His Highest.* New York: Dodd, Mead and Co., 1935.

Dickens, Charles. *A Tale of Two Cities. The Works of Charles Dickens.* Vol. 13. New York: Peter Fenelon Collier, nd.

Emerson, Ralph Waldo. *American Poetry and Prose.* Ed. Norman Foerster. Fifth ed. Part One. Boston: Houghton Mifflin, 1970.

Everyman. The Norton Anthology of World Masterpieces. Ed. Maynard Mack. Sixth ed. Vol. 1. New York: Norton, 1992.

Foster, Richard J. *The Celebration of Discipline.* San Francisco: Harper and Row, 1978.

Galloway, Dale. *Dream a New Dream: How to Rebuild a Broken Life.* Wheaton, IL: Tyndale House, 1975.

Halasz, Nicholas. Qtd. in *Creative Brooding* by Robert A. Raines. New York: Macmillan, 1966.

Hemingway, Ernest. *The Sun Also Rises.* New York: Charles Scribner's Sons, 1926.

The Holy Bible. Revised Standard Version. New York: Thomas Nelson: 1952.

The Hymnal 1982. New York: The Church Hymnal Corporation, 1985.

James, P. D. *The Black Tower.* New York: Popular Library, 1975.

Job. The NIV/KJV Parallel Bible. Grand Rapids, MI: Zondervan, 1985.

The Norton Anthology of World Masterpieces. Ed. Maynard Mack. Sixth ed. Vol. 1. New York: Norton, 1992.

Kempis, Thomas a. *The Imitation of Christ.* Westwood, NJ: The Christian Library, 1984.

Lange, Hermann. *Dying We Live.* Eds. Helmut Gollwitzer, Kathe Kuhn, Reinhold Schneider. Reinhold C. Kuhn, trans. New York: Pantheon, 1956.

Law, William. *A Serious Call to a Devout and Holy Life.* Ed. John W. Meister. Philadelphia: Westminster, 1955.

Lewis, C. S. *Surprised by Joy.* New York: Harcourt, Brace & World, 1955.

Milton, John. *Paradise Lost.* Major British Writers. Ed. G. B. Harrison. Vol. 1. New York: Harcourt, Brace, 1959.

Neuman, Matthias, O. S. B. "Learning to Forgive Yourself." *Care Notes.* St. Meinrad, IN: Abbey Press, 1991.

Newton, John. Qtd. in *The Anglican Digest.* Lent, 1996. 29.

Nouwen, Henri J. M. *Making All Things New: An Invitation to the Spiritual Life.* San Francisco: Harper and Row, 1981.

————. *Reaching Out.* Garden City, NY: Doubleday, 1975.

O'Connor, Flannery. *The Complete Stories.* New York: Farrar, Straus & Giroux, 1946.

O'Driscoll, Herbert. *Prayers for the Breaking of Bread: Meditations on the Collects of the Church Year.* Cambridge, Boston, MA: Cowley Pub., 1991.

Seamands, David A. *Healing of Memories.* USA, Canada, England: Victor Books, 1986.

Works Cited

Shelley, Mary. *Frankenstein*. Signet Classic. New York: New American Library, 1965.

Tolstoy, Leo. "The Death of Ivaan Ilych." *The Story and Its Writer*. Ed. Ann Charters. Third ed. Boston: Bedford Books of St. Martin's Press, 1991.

Wheeler, Mark. *Lord, Make Us Instruments of Thy Will!* Holy Trinity Episcopal Church, Lenten Devotional, 1996.

Wilson, A. N. *Writers Revealed*. Ed. Rosemary Hartill. New York: Peter Bedrick Books, 1989.